# SANTA FE
*Seduction*

SIZZLING CITY SERIES
BOOK 1

## ZIZI HART

SECRET
PASSAGE PRESS, LLC

Santa Fe Seduction
Copyright © 2024 by Zizi Hart.
Published by Secret Passage Press, LLC

This book is a work of fiction. Names, characters,
places, and incidents either are products of the author's
imagination or are used fictitiously. Any resemblance to actual events
or locales or persons, living or dead, is entirely coincidental.
All rights reserved. No part of this book may be used or reproduced
in any manner whatsoever without written permission
except in the case of brief quotations embodied
in critical articles or reviews.

For information contact:
www.zizihart.com
www.secretpassage-press.com

Cover design by Miranda Lexa
Editing by Robert Ladd

ISBN: 978-1-9644-6000-0 (paperback)
ISBN: 978-1-9644-6001-7 (hardcover)
ISBN: 978-1-9644-6002-4 (eBook)

First Edition: April 2024

Secret Passage Press, LLC
Canon City, CO

## *Disclaimer*

This book contains adult language, themes, and sexually explicit scenes.
It is intended for readers 18+.

*To Tamara.*
*My inspiration. My cheerleader. My Bestie.*
*Thanks for all your support.*
*I couldn't have done this without you*

# SANTA FE SEDUCTION

## Chapter 1

*Cruz*

Bright security lights blasted through my windshield as I made the painfully slow creeping turn in the fast-food drive-thru. I squinted at the diabolical glowing orbs and let loose a series of curse words in Spanish. I didn't care that my window was open and others in line could hear me. I was exhausted from my shift bartending at Club Cuervo and equally frustrated with the lack of success from accomplishing my goals, those I could tell no one about. I rifled through my glove box searching for the case and slipped on my shades. What was taking so damn long? Breakfast burritos. That's all I wanted. And to get a few hours of sleep before diving into my real job. But choices were limited at 3am, and I refused to pull out of line and go home empty handed. I had nothing edible in the fridge. I closed my eyes, compelling the cars in front of me to move. I blinked them open. Of course, it hadn't worked. I blew out a breath, trying to relax my muscles, rolling my neck, attempting to find my Zen, as my favorite sister Sofía always told me. She was into all that woo-woo spiritual crap, that I told her I didn't have time for. Stress is a killer, she would say in that bossy tone of hers, meditation is good for the body and mind. I could almost hear her voice now. I cracked a smile. Sofía didn't understand my job, actually no one in my family did. I was thankful for their ignorance. Mi mamá and sisters would worry endlessly. Still no movement from the cars ahead. I visualized ramming into them like in one of those crime video games. I pinched the bridge of my nose and closed my eyes again. Breathe in. Breathe out. Try not to ram into the cars in front of me. I tried to channel some of my sister's patience.

My Ford Mustang was suddenly wrenched forward. What the Fuck? Had the idiot behind me been battling the same urge? The beat-up Honda Civic with bug-splattered windows was the one that bumped me, but no one was driving. Where the hell was the driver? I bolted out my door, whipping off my shades as I stormed to the little POS. Somebody was going to pay. This was exactly what I needed to burn off a little excess rage. A head popped up in the driver's seat for a moment and then bobbed back down again.

"Hey dumbass." I said leaning down into the open window. "You just hit my car."

Yeah, I was stating the obvious, but I didn't care. I was itching for a fight. This asshole couldn't do what I had just been thinking about doing to the car in front of me. I was a hypocrite, but I didn't give....

A sexy brunette flipped back her hair to reveal bedroom eyes with long curly lashes. It made me hesitate. I wanted to bite back my words. Her eyes roamed my body slowly, devouring the sight. She spent time admiring the tats covering my arms and shoulders. My biceps flexed in response. She gave a sharp intake of breath. Yeah. She liked what she saw. Not a surprise. That's how women usually responded. Her gaze finally crawled up to my eyes and scowled. Hmm. Not typical. Most women said I had the face of an angel. Not that I'm conceited at all.

"Back the eff up mister."

She shoved at my arm, trying to move me back, but I easily stood my ground. Somehow, I found her efforts amusing.

# SANTA FE SEDUCTION

"Personal space. You're in it." She growled.

I grinned. I always liked women with attitude. They were way more fun in bed. She held my stare and waited. I debated for a second, then took a step back and crossed my arms. She focused lower on my body. I wondered if and when she would realize that testing me was a mistake. I looked like a typical gang banger with my sleeveless tank. My silk over-shirt was still on my passenger seat, exactly where I had thrown it, the moment I left work. Her eyes darkened as she watched the sweat roll down my chest to add to my already damp shirt. The hot-blooded brunette was interested, but she was fighting it. I should make it easy on her.

"Your number. I want it."

"Hell no." She responded. It seemed automatic, but the spark in her eyes gave her away. I think she thought I was hitting on her. Which. I was. Sort of. I wasn't exactly at my best at 3am.

"You got insurance?"

"Bu-but, I barely touched your stupid sports car." She sputtered. The woman glanced through her windshield and winced. Our cars were still plastered together. You could barely make out the Mach 1 on the rear bumper.

The truck behind her started beeping its horn. Of course, the line started moving the moment I wanted to explore where this conversation might go. I gave the truck driver a scowl and climbed into my car to move up the single car-length. I jumped out again. This discussion was far from over. I glanced at my rear bumper before approaching her car. It was just a few scratches, something I could probably buff out and paint myself. Not that I'd tell her that.

The brunette had her head under the dash again. What was it with this chica? Had she dropped something? My curiosity got the better of me.

"Get out of the car." I knew my gravelly voice was harsh. It was demanding. I was used to barking orders and those around me, obeying my commands.

# ZIZI HART

Another scowl, but her eyes softened. "I can't." She pleaded.

What did that mean? Was she embarrassed by her rumpled clothes, or lack of makeup? Her over-sized ripped sweatshirt and skinny jeans looked cute from what I could see. Her long chestnut hair was tangled and wind-swept, like she had driven with the windows down for hours. The freshly fucked hairstyle worked for me. It was sexy as hell and sending my mind down dirty roads with endless possibilities. Crumpled wrappers and receipts littered her passenger seat. Her green eyes continued to stare at me with defiance. The truck behind her honked again.

I launched myself at the truck, growling, "If you honk that thing one more fucking time, so help me, I will rip you one."

The beefy man in the cowboy hat put his hands up. I knew my glare could be menacing when I wanted it to be. At least the driver of the F-350 had some smarts.

I turned back to her smirking, "Phone number. Now." It was an order. Not a request.

She huffed and scribbled her number on a receipt, swearing under her breath.

"Fine." She slapped the paper into my outstretched hand.

I held onto her fingertips for a moment before allowing her to snatch her hand back with a yank.

My mouth quirked. Most women responded to my sex appeal, but this one was different. Getting a women's number had never been so hard, or quite so satisfying. I glanced at the number she scribbled down on the receipt before sliding it into my wallet. Her name was Mari. Cute. I strolled back to my car slowly, letting her check out my backside. I turned to give her a wink, but she wasn't paying attention. Her head had ducked beneath the dash again. I climbed into my car and pulled forward. Instead of leaving directly after getting my food, I parked and watched her get her order and drive away. I snapped a photo of her license plate. She was from Arizona. Not that it mattered. I had friends

# SANTA FE SEDUCTION

that could track her down, even if she had given me a bogus phone number.

    I started making my way home noticing that the woman matched my route, turn for turn. Her driving was erratic, with jerky movements and inconsistent speeds. If I didn't know better, I would have thought she was drunk. Then she turned down the street I lived on. This was getting more interesting by the minute. She pulled into the apartment complex next to mine. Chipped paint, dented doors, and perilous stairways made up the complex décor. My apartment wasn't a whole lot better but at least the landlord was trying. He had recently given all the buildings a fresh coat of paint, covering the majority of graffiti that seemed to plague most of the buildings in the neighborhood. I watched as she juggled her food, backpack, and a bulky cardboard box. I debated briefly if I should stop and help, but she'd probably think I was a stalker, instead of it just being a coincidence that we lived close by. I watched as she bounded up the steps to the $2^{nd}$ floor and snapped a pic of her apartment number. What the Fuck? She was heading into BJ's apartment, the guy who had OD'd two weeks ago. The landlord must have rented it already.

    I drove one lot over and parked in front of my building thinking about the guy that died. BJ had worked with me at the Club. He had been my bar-back, a hard-working scrawny guy. Kind of twitchy, but drugs made most people paranoid. He had seemed more on edge a few days before. I felt guilty when he passed. Not that I had anything to do with his death, at least not directly. But I couldn't help but feel like I had been a cog in the wheel. His was one of the faces that kept me up most nights. My insomnia was the result of a lot of demons. They had plagued my soul for too many years. My apartment faced his balcony. It hadn't been a coincidence. I had been paid to keep tabs on him. He was valuable. A tool. I tried to convince myself that I couldn't have done anything to prevent what happened. I had been working at the club that night. I spent the last two weeks going over everything in my mind. BJ had been stirring up trouble, and those that did, ended up dead. Half a year at the club, and I had learned how things worked. Sometimes, I wondered what would have happened if I had warned him. Would it have saved him? Or would I have just added to the body count? The police came by the club to ask questions. They didn't spend much time investigating. The owner wanted the whole incident to go away, and he had influential friends. The official file said it was an accidental overdose. My gut told me otherwise. Not that it mattered. There was no proof, and the guy was a known user.

    I unlocked my apartment keeping the lights off and opened the blinds to the patio staring into the apartment across the parking lot. The shadows of the sexy brunette bounced off the unopened blinds. She moved, just like her driving. Wild. All that energy. I couldn't help but grin. It took effort to force my gaze from the blinds. I had little time for women. Things were ramping up, and I had to focus. I tamped down my libido. Food. Sleep. And research. Nothing would stop me from reaching my goal, no matter how sexy or sweet.

# Chapter 2

*Mari*

Trying to balance everything while unlocking the apartment was a feat, I thought I deserved a medal for. I got inside the apartment and flipped on the lights. Benjie's clothes were thrown haphazardly around the room. Piles were on the floor and coffee table. A few dirty dishes in the sink. I had disposed of old pizza boxes and fast-food wrappers when I had visited his apartment two weeks ago to plan the funeral. Benjie had always been a bit of a slob. Even as kids he never kept his room clean. But something was off. The apartment looked worse than last time. Goosebumps traveled up my arms despite the stifling heat in the apartment. Drawers were pulled out from the furniture, and the contents strewn across the floor like someone had been looking for something. I set the box on the tile and my food and backpack on the kitchen table. I grabbed my heavy flashlight from my pack and held it in front of me like a bat as I searched the apartment. While shuffling through the debris, I wondered if I should call the cops. Not that my experience with the Santa Fe PD had filled me with confidence. Detective Dillon had said Benjie's death was an accident, and refused to investigate further. But there were too many things that didn't add up. I had gotten a cryptic text message

# ZIZI HART

the day he died. Last week I received a coded journal from him in the mail, and now his place was trashed. Was that enough for the police to finally do something? Could I even trust them?

It didn't take long to realize that no one was there. It was a small apartment with few places to hide. Nothing looked like it had been stolen. The TV and stereo were still on its stand. Even some loose bills on the nightstand looked untouched. I bolted the front door and angled the back of a kitchen chair under the knob. I didn't know if it would really prevent someone from coming in, but at least it would alert me if someone tried. I flipped on the air conditioning and was grateful when cool air flowed. I realized that I had no clue if utilities came with the rent, or if I needed to pay that separately. I should have asked the property manager a lot more questions when I had picked up the keys and set up the sublet. Not that I had been all that capable at the time. I wasn't a lot better now. I had been mostly a zombie these past few weeks, but I needed answers. That's why I had made the decision to drive down from Tempe, Arizona. I needed to pack up Benjie's apartment and figure out what really happened.

I opened up the box I had brought in, and a ball of black and white fluff leapt out and scrambled across the kitchen floor. It hid by the kick-board under the kitchen cabinets. It was probably a male by the amount of trouble it gave me. I wondered how old the kitten was. I didn't have much experience with them growing up. My step-dad would never have allowed us to have a pet. His whole purpose in life seemed to be making my life and Benjie's as miserable as possible. He excelled at that job.

I let the kitten get used to his surrounding, while I searched through the cabinets. In one I found a single can of tuna. In another, was a mis-matched set of chipped plates, glasses, and bowls. I pulled two small bowls out, filling one with water, and the other with tuna. The cat peeked from its hiding spot when I used the can opener. Its little nose sniffed the air like crazy. I didn't want to scare the little guy more than he already was. I set

## SANTA FE SEDUCTION

the bowls down on the floor and walked to the couch with my bag of food. I pretended to focus on a magazine while munching on my breakfast burrito. He kept glancing back at me while sniffing the contents of the bowl. He gave a tentative lick and his eyes closed in bliss. No longer caring about anything else, he dove into the food like he was starving. I had stopped at a gas station about half-way between Tempe and Santa Fe. He had been peeking around the pump, covered in oil and grease, panting and scared. The attendant said he was a stray that had been wandering around the area for a few days. I had asked for a towel and a box to try and catch him. That must have been quite the entertainment for the guy watching. I had slipped on some oil, knocked over several cans, and fell a number of times while chasing the little guy. I had bumps and bruises from the whole ordeal. A bubble of laughter burst past my lips, imagining a video of me posted somewhere on the internet racing around the gas station. In the end, I had been victorious, capturing the cute little critter without any bites or scratches. Another feat I believed I deserved a medal for. The little guy had escaped from the box a few times during the drive. He obviously didn't like being cooped up. I couldn't blame him. I knew it was hard to trust. I had learned from experience.

"I'm with you buddy." I held my soda in the air, toasting the kitten.

He had been cleaning his paws after devouring his dinner, or was it breakfast? He paused for a moment, in mid tongue swipe and tilted his head. I shook mine. Did he even realize how absolutely adorable he was? I smiled despite myself. It had been weeks since I had cracked a grin. The muscles felt tight in my cheeks. Experiencing any happiness, just seemed wrong. I don't understand why death makes you feel that way. Over the past few weeks, guilt seemed to claw at my insides until I could barely breathe. That's why I was here. For Benjie and for closure.

I watched as the kitten finished cleaning himself, and then with a full belly, curl up in a particularly fluffy pile of Benjie's

clothes. A tear slid down my cheek. Benjie would have fallen in love with the little guy. I let out a sigh. The scariest part of the whole trip, wasn't the long drive at night, it had been when the kitten had gotten under the brake pedal. Luckily that hadn't happened while driving down the freeway. I gave a shudder thinking about that possibility. It was only at the drive thru when I had rolled into that fancy sports car. I didn't want to accidentally step on the kitten, who was so small and skinny, despite all the fluff. That jerk hadn't even given me a chance to explain.
"Effing Bastard."
The kitten looked at me, concern on his face.
"Don't worry. I'm not talking about you. It was that guy at the drive through."
He had been all bossy, and intimidating, with those dark brooding blood-shot eyes, and scary tats. His shoulder-length deep sable mane was as untamed as his attitude. Why were the dreamy guys always such dicks? I had gotten distracted by his gorgeous bod. It looked like it had been carved from stone. Honestly, that man's body should be in a museum. I closed my eyes imagining him standing on a pedestal naked, behind a gold-plated chain to keep the public away. Mmm. I'd pay to see that exhibit. The figure in my mind turned to face me. It spoke. No. Not spoke. It yelled at me. Just like the real one had. I shivered remembering the intense energy he had projected. I sighed. He would have been perfect, if he had just kept his mouth shut. I wish I had ripped into him, like he did to the driver behind me. Normally I would have, but I just didn't have the energy after the long trip. It was probably for the best. He might have been an even bigger asshole. I wondered briefly what astronomical amount he would come up with to fix his precious car.
"You're already more trouble than you're worth." I pointed at the kitten. It stared back at me and tilted his head. "Aww. You're way too cute. I can't stay mad at you."

# SANTA FE SEDUCTION

I gave a huge yawn. It was time to get some rest. I made a quick trip to the hallway bathroom to freshen up before bed. The kitten stopped in to visit as I was finishing up. He eyed the toilet paper roll. He looked at me over his shoulder as if gauging my reaction. I stared back. He spun the roll until half of it lay on the floor. I think he was daring me to react. When I didn't do or say anything, he walked past me to the bedroom. I followed along grinning at his lovable antics. We were a perfect pair. If I had any doubts before, they were now long gone. I watched him climb the huge bed, with his sharp kitten claws digging into the bedspread. He kneaded the pillow at the head of the bed until he was satisfied before settling down with a yawn. I followed suit, yawning long and loud. There was so much I wanted to get done, and now I needed to add things for the cat, to my growing list of items to pick up. Listening to the soft purr of the kitten, made me realize how exhausted I was. After some sleep, I'd be able to concentrate on other stuff. Until then, everything could wait. I climbed in, careful not to disturb the kitten's rest atop the only pillow in the bed. I wadded up my sweatshirt creating my own pillow and snuggled under the covers. It didn't take long for my mind to quiet and fade into sleep next to my newfound pal.

    I woke a few hours later, with a furry face staring at me. He was on my chest watching. I blinked at the bright light streaming through the blinds wondering how long he had been waiting. I groaned. "What time is it?" I turned to find the clock. Wiping the sleep from my eyes, I read the time. It was a little after 7. Great. Three whole hours of sleep. The kitten seemed raring to go. I wondered if he was already hungry again.

    Glancing at the bedspread covered in tiny dirt paw prints, I wondered if I should have spent some time cleaning him up before going to bed. The oil stains would probably never come out, not that the bedspread was anything special. Everything in Benjie's apartment looked like it had been bought from a thrift store.

# ZIZI HART

"Are you hungry for another breakfast little guy?"

The kitten seemed to know exactly what I meant and did some strange little leaping dance on the bed. I picked him up and set him on the floor and the kitten sprinted to the kitchen, his claws slipping and sliding across the tile floor, as he spun and tumbled into the water dish. He gave me a perplexed expression, his fur dripping.

"Are you soaking wet?" I grabbed the kitchen towel and carefully dried him off. He seemed to realize I was there to help him. Peering into the rest of the cabinets, I didn't find much. The lack of basic grocery items, gave my heart a pang. Could Benjie not afford food? Or was he just the typical bachelor that always ate out? I was really hoping for the latter. I should have reached out to check on him more often. I guess I wasn't a very good sister. The tuna can I had opened last night, was the only one I could find. The pet store run moved to the top of my list, as his heartbreaking stare greeted mine over the empty food bowl.

"I know. I gotta get more food."

He meowed loudly.

"I'm going to take that as agreement."

I looked up the closest pet stores on my phone and told Miles to stay. I had picked his name this morning. I had driven for miles and miles and found him on my way. It fit. I briefly wondered what the apartment would look like when I returned. Although, the cat could hardly make it look worse than it already was.

Returning with new linens, groceries, and all manner of cat essentials, I was greeted with a puddle at the door. I sighed. The kitten ducked under the couch. Did he think he was in trouble? That made me sad that the little guy was so worried. What kind of abuse had Miles already had in his short life? I closed the door and locked it, setting down my bags and cleaned up the mess with a spare towel. I set up the litter box in the bathroom and encouraged the kitten into the box with treats. It

# SANTA FE SEDUCTION

took a few tries, but the kitten enjoyed digging in the litter and making a mess with the sand.

I poured some dry cat food in the bowl. It obviously wasn't as exciting as the tuna. He sniffed the contents and decided it was acceptable and started munching. I unwrapped another breakfast burrito I had picked up on the way back to the apartment. My brother had always made fun of my metabolism. I could eat more than him and not gain a pound. He wasn't a whole lot bigger than me, but he never had my appetite. Although that could have been a side-effect from the drugs. I shoved the paperwork from the coffee table off to the side to make room for my bag remembering how we used to be when growing up. So many emotions flooded my mind, sorrow, anger, regret. I hadn't really let myself grieve these last two weeks, ever since Benjie died. The kitten decided to come investigate. He climbed up my jeans and shirt and rested on my shoulder snuggling into my neck as he watched me bring the burrito up to my mouth. He put a paw on my cheek leaning in to sniff it as I took my first bite.

"I take it, you want some?"

He meowed. It filled my aching heart with something I couldn't identify, but it loosened the tightness in my chest. I shared my burrito with this crazy adorable kitten, because I couldn't share it with my brother. He was gone. Someone had taken him away from me, because I refused to believe it had been an accident. And when I found that person, they were going to pay.

As exhausted as I still was, I was going to attempt the unthinkable and try to give the kitten a bath. It wasn't going to be pretty. I closed the bathroom door when he followed me in and filled the sink with warm water. I bought some Dawn dish soap to help with the oil, on a suggestion from the pet store clerk. The curious kitten watched from the counter as the water filled. He swiped one paw at the running water. It was now or never. I gently wrapped him in a wash cloth covering his claws and delicately rubbed his fur with soap, giving him encouragement.

"It's ok little guy. It will be over soon, and you can take a nice long nap."

The kitten was desperate to get out of the water at first, squirming and clawing, screaming its displeasure, but it would pause every time I spoke. Once every last bit of dirt and grime was gone, I towel-dried the little guy and placed him on the bedroom floor. After stripping the bed, I found a dry towel and bundled him in it. His little face poked out of the wadded towel shivering. He was mad at me. I got that.

"My brother never liked baths either. But I don't care. You were filthy. Be furious all you want. You needed it."

I looked at the dirty bedding and all the clothes and sighed wondering if there was anything I could salvage from this mess, or if I should just toss it all. I settled on opening the box of garbage bags, and threw everything into bags. Clean first. Sort later. It gave me something to focus on, and sad to say, but I was grateful for the distraction. Tonight, I'd be visiting Benjie's last known place of work, Club Cuervo. My stomach was tied up in knots. I knew I needed answers. My guilt compelled me to get to the truth. No matter how ugly it turned out to be.

# Chapter 3

*Cruz*

The music was thumping like a heavy pulse as the patrons of Club Cuervo grinded up against one another. The DJ's lights flashed like a spinning patrol car. The women were dressed from skank to chic, while men plied them with liquor. It kept me busy, doling out drinks to the savages. Not that I wasn't just like one of those other men. I'd be equally invested in scoring if the right woman walked in, or the wrong woman for that matter. Not that I would have gotten serious with any of them. It had been years since that happened. Long before I had worked at this club. But a one-night stand I could do, and had done plenty of nights these last six months. I was a flirt, but then that was part of the job. I worked for tips as a bartender, but I also did some side work to boost sales. Taking home the occasional patron wasn't a problem, as long as it didn't affect the business. Club Cuervo's owner, Luís Lorenzo aka El Lobo Rojo, knew my value, and what I could accomplish. He was just beginning to really trust me, and bring me in on more of the operation. He enjoyed watching my extra-curricular activities, so I played my part and put on a show.

The song changed to something sweet, and a few people on the dance floor groaned and went back to their tables. That's when she walked in. I barely recognized her from this morning. Mari strolled in with sexy silver stilettos and a skin tight red dress that had more than one man turning his head, along with several woman. She flipped her long dark locks over her shoulder and made her way to the bar. A waitress was rattling off a drink order, but I wasn't paying attention. My brain couldn't focus on anything but the woman in red. I stared. She slid into a bar seat and casually looked around.

"Come on Cruz. Stop staring at the animals. A Cosmo and 3 drafts." Rosa slapped her hand on the sticky bar, drawing my attention.

I smiled. Rosa often referred to the customers as animals in a zoo. It was a fitting analogy. Most of the people were little more than base urges. I mixed the Cosmo, poured the beers and sent Rosa out into the wild. I grinned at the swish of her hips, as she meandered across the dance floor avoiding drunks, and swatting away unwanted advances. I turned my attention back to Mari. She still hadn't noticed me. I grabbed the drink specials menu and slid it in front of her. She focused on the colorful page of concoctions.

"See anything you like?" I leaned against the neon-lit bar and smiled. I knew how the light and shadows danced across my forearms in-time with the beat of the bass. Her eyes crawled up my torso so slowly, I felt like I was being stripped bare in front of her. I didn't mind it one bit. She drew in large gulps of air and held her breath.

"You."

My grin grew. "Yeah?"

She looked around the bar at the other patrons, like she would find an ally among them. Good luck Mari. They were all out for themselves.

"I can't believe you work here."

"It's not that big of a town. Guess I don't need to track you down."

# SANTA FE SEDUCTION

She swallowed. "Did you already get an estimate for the damages?"

"Not yet." I wasn't about to have her pay a dime for the repairs, but that didn't mean I couldn't string her along just for fun of it.

She made some kind of grumbling noise. I couldn't make out the words under her breath, but I bet they were all swear words. It made me smile brighter.

Another customer at the end of the bar was waving me over. I ignored him, concentrating my full attention on Mari. I knew I couldn't do that for long, but I didn't want to end this conversation just yet. The night had gotten interesting.

"How long have you been working here?"

I tilted my head. It was an odd question. "You mean tonight?"

"No. I meant when did you start working at Club Cuervo?"

"You a cop?"

She blanched. "Me?"

I nodded. It was a fair question. We didn't get many people in that asked personal questions. Anyone interested in employee details was begging for trouble. That was a big no-no in this business. Luís didn't like anyone nosing around, moving in on his territory. It was dangerous to get on his bad side. His temper was legendary. She definitely wasn't any kind of law enforcement. She didn't the temperament for it, and I knew most of those on the local force. Only one personally, but the rest I had files on. Luís had records as well, and contacts. He used information as leverage to get them to do anything he wanted. He was ruthless. She's not one of his competitors either. That would guarantee her a death sentence. She had innocence stamped across her forehead, despite her sexy get-up. I glanced around the club, following the line of sight from various predators all leering at her from various vantage points. I didn't know why, but I felt the need

# ZIZI HART

to protect her. She didn't seem to have a clue of her surroundings. Lack of situational awareness could be hazardous to your health.

"Stop chatting up the girl, and get us some beers." The guy at the end of the bar said.

He must have had enough of my delays. I hesitated for a moment, but gave in and supplied him with his order. It was still early enough in the evening where it wasn't that busy. A few of the predators prowled closer to Mari. I needed to make it clear, she was off limits.

My barback, Ramón came alongside me and jabbed his elbow into my ribs while I stared at Mari.

"Oof. Whadya do that for?"

Ramón chuckled. "Your ojos popped out of your cabeza. Dude."

I rubbed my side. I hadn't even heard him, and here I was thinking Mari's situational awareness sucked. She was a distraction I didn't need.

"A new conquest?" Ramón asked.

I shrugged. I don't know why the question grated on my nerves. Was that how they all saw me? Another predator among the many in the club. It shouldn't bother me. But I guess I hadn't really shown another side of my personality to my co-workers. They saw me as a one-trick pony, because that's exactly what I portrayed. To save Mari from the vultures, my rep might just come in handy.

"Ramón. You wanna tend bar while I make a move?"

"No way. You give me chance? I won't let you down. I study that mixology libro you gave me."

I knew that Ramón had been wanting to bartend ever since he showed up. His English wasn't the best, but he really enjoyed mixing drinks. I had been teaching him during our down-time.

Ramón kept prattling on, but I had already walked away, wanting to reach Mari before any sleazy characters made their

# SANTA FE SEDUCTION

way over. I slipped out from behind the bar, and stepped in front of a regular. I stared him down, and he slunk back to his table.

"We weren't properly introduced this morning. My name is Cruz." I delicately lifted her hand to my lips and tilted my head giving her my best piercing stare. It was an old-fashioned gesture that seemed to work wonders on most woman.

Mari's chest inhaled filling out her sexy strapless dress. I could tell she didn't know how to react.

"Would you do me the honor of a dance?"

I didn't give her a chance to respond before ushering her out onto the dance floor. She squeaked an incoherent reply and before she knew it, we were gliding across the floor in a tango. I had been a dance instructor for a few years before moving onto bigger and better things. It had come in handy, just like it did now. It might have been a dick move, not giving her a choice, but it got results. And when something worked, it worked.

## Chapter 4

*Mari*

Who was this character? He was suave and sexy and an incredible dancer, but I shouldn't care about any of that. I should hate him. He was the pompous ass who would be charging me a fortune for barely tapping his precious sports car. But the way he stared into my eyes, like I was the only woman on the planet. It confused the hell out of me. I felt mesmerized as he glided us around on the dance floor. I forced myself to blink. I knew better than to fall for some guy I just met. It had to be an act. I'm sure this was how he scored. He was a good actor. Oscar-worthy, in fact. It had given me pause, even questioning my own emotions. I knew this supposed passion I was feeling was pure lust. Nothing more than that. It wasn't real. The question was, what was his motive? He gave a nudge to my hand, steering us both into a turn. It was like our bodies had been made for one another. The Latin music intensified the electricity I felt down to my toes. The song ended, and he held me close. He spoke no words, just an intense stare that had my stomach doing flip-flops. Even though I knew in the back of my mind, this was a bad idea, I decided to give in. What could it hurt? If I flirted back with this outrageous bartender, just to see where things went. I definitely needed information, and he might be the best source in the place.

I slid my hand lower down his waist, and shifted closer. His lips parted for a moment. Our hips were almost touching. I could feel the heat from his body. My eyelids fluttered. It was such a tease, in this position. I could tell he wanted me, and I definitely wanted him, despite the growing list of reasons why I shouldn't. I hadn't had a drop of alcohol and already felt light-headed. We danced to three more songs before we were both panting from the electric chemistry that pulsed between us. He had to be just as turned on as I was. He sat me at the bar, and I asked him questions, whispering in his ear. He whispered his answers back, his breath tickling the hairs on my neck. I shivered as he touched my shoulder and leaned in. I couldn't concentrate when he did that.

"So, how long have you been bartending?"

"It feels like forever."

"Does that mean you don't like working here?"

"It's a job."

"Did you know Benjie Jones? I think he went by BJ. He worked as a barback."

Cruz didn't answer. Instead, he introduced me to his barback, Ramón. Maybe he hadn't heard the question correctly. The club's music was pretty loud. Cruz disappeared, and Ramón in turn introduced me to some very strong libations. After three drinks, I weaved through the club and barely made it to the bathroom. A cocktail waitress joined me at the sink while I applied more lipstick. Her name was Rosa. We chatted for several minutes. About what I couldn't tell you. She seemed super nice, although by this point everyone seemed friendly. I had quite the buzz going.

When I got back to the bar, Cruz was behind it, and serving drinks. I was a little disappointed, but I guess he was working. I bet his boss wouldn't appreciate him flirting all night. Then that's exactly what he started doing. Soft touches and whispers as he

# SANTA FE SEDUCTION

doled out drinks to women left and right. They flirted right back. Some of them more blatant than others. I tried not to be mad at him, but jealousy reared its ugly head. Logic didn't seem to matter. I tried to convince myself that Cruz was a lost cause. He hadn't been all that forthcoming with answers to my questions anyhow. So, I started showing Benjie's picture around to see if anyone else recognized him. Ramón said that he didn't know him but he had only been working at the club a few weeks. He suggested I ask Cruz since he had been working at the club for months now. Ramón continued to supply me with free cocktails. He told me I was his official taste tester for the evening. Cruz seemed upset when I went around asking others about Benjie, especially other guys. Was he jealous? What was this high school? We had only just met. He didn't own me.

"I don't think you should be asking any more questions." Cruz said through gritted teeth.

"Why?" I asked, trying to focus on his eyes, but failing. I suddenly wanted to rub against his chest for a while. That sounded like a fabulous idea.

I leaned in and grabbed his face, running my fingers along his sexy stubble. I turned his head and yelled in his ear. "Are you jealous of me talking to other men?"

He shook his head. "You're being a nuisance."

I smoothed my hands down the front of my dress, wiping off invisible dust. "And you're being a dick. I don't care if you are sexy as sin."

I made another trip to the bathroom. It took way too much effort to walk a straight line. I needed to refrain from any more of Ramón's specials. They were making my head spin one way, and the bar the another.

I bumped into Rosa again.

"How are you doing girl?"

"Fiiiinne." I nodded. Losing my balance and catching myself before face-planting on the bathroom counter.

# ZIZI HART

"Uh huh. Maybe you should switch to water about now."

"I think you're right. I need my wits about me. I've made a decision. I'm going to seduce the bartender. He has something I want."

Rosa laughed. "You, and a lot of girls."

I frowned. Were more people wanting to get info about Benjie from him? That didn't make a whole lot of sense. Why would anyone else care? I shook my head realizing it didn't matter.

With my mission decided, I trudged through the gyrating bodies on the dance floor and plopped my butt onto the barstool and focused all my energy on the sexiest man in the club. Cruz. The misogynistic asshole, and the key to everything I had been searching for. At least I hoped.

# Chapter 5

*Cruz*

Mari was hammered. Whatever cocktails Ramón had dreamed up, had knocked her on her ass, literally. She had barely made it to the barstool. At least she had stopped showing BJ's picture to everyone in the place. It was causing a scene. Was BJ an ex-lover? What was he to Mari? Yeah. It made me a little jealous even though I had no reason to be. We had met less than 24 hours ago. I was grateful she started asking for water, and stayed put, but I could tell she was fading fast. Her cute little butt would be sliding right off that barstool pretty soon. It was almost closing time, and I knew what that meant. The men who hadn't hooked up would be on the hunt for prey. I wasn't about to let Mari fall victim to those vultures.

"Last call." I announced.

Any men who attempted to approach Mari were met by my glare and backed away. Even the drunk bastards took one look, and turned tail and ran.

Rosa took off her shoes and stretched her feet on a chair and counted her tips. Mari's head was now slumped over in a bowl of pretzels, and it was one of the cutest things I had ever seen.

"You gonna wake her up?" Rosa asked.

"Not yet." I grinned.

Rosa shook her head. "You know she bragged about seducing you."

I tilted my head and stared at the softly snoring vixen in red. "I guess it worked since I'm taking her home."

"Pretzel face? Is that some sort of new fetish you're into?" I laughed. "Ramón, can you finish up?"

"Sure thing." He grinned. Ramón knew I was a ladies' man. I took a different one home almost every night. There was nothing odd about that, although until now, they had always been conscious.

I picked up Mari and made my way through the club. My boss stopped me before the back door with raised brows. It pissed me off how put together he was at the end of the night. Sweat dripped down my shirt causing dark circles to appear under my pits. My hair stuck up at crazy angles, and here Luís Lorenzo stood in a silk suit without a single wrinkle. His tie was perfectly straight. Slicked backed salt and pepper hair matched a neatly trimmed beard and mustache. I knew the image was partly for his political contacts and the media, but he was also anal retentive in the extreme, a complete neat freak. He had to keep extra suits in his office, because the word was, El Lobo Rojo didn't mind getting his hands dirty. Not that I had seen it firsthand, but those rumors had earned him a reputation and a nickname that fit. The amount of blood on this man's hands made me sick. It frustrated me how respectable he always appeared. Underneath the immaculate silk suit lived a monster. He pretended to give back to the community, helping those with drug addictions, when he was nothing but a drug lord. My stomach churned. I forced a smile and hoped it masked the utter disgust I had for the man.

"Luís." I nodded.

He eyed the girl in my arms, studying her like a specimen. It was creepy as hell, and it made me want to hold her tighter, curl her into my chest, but I knew that would only make him want her

# SANTA FE SEDUCTION

more, so I tried to look casual and not show the tension climbing my spine.

"Do you have the receipts from tonight?" Luís asked.

"I gave them to Ramón."

"Is he ready?"

I shrugged. Non-committal. I didn't know what to say. Ramón was Luís' nephew. The kid was family. He was a decent kid, from a rotten family. Did I think he could do what Luís did? No. Hell, no. But I wasn't about to share that knowledge with him.

"I'll leave you to your... entertainment."

I didn't like how he used that word and what it implied. I blew out a breath when I got to the car. Any interaction with El Lobo Rojo was scary, no matter how mundane. I was grateful to get out of there unscathed. You never knew how he would react. I briefly wondered what word he was going to say before he reconsidered.

I got Mari buckled in and drove to her place. I wasn't about to have her in my apartment, not until I learned more about her. How she knew BJ for starters and why she was asking so many questions. I told myself it had nothing to do with jealousy and everything to do with survival. Questions got you killed. And Mari's good looks would only get her so far. I looted through her purse and found her keys. She was still passed out. Luckily, I knew her apartment number by heart. I climbed the steps with her in my arms with ease. Unlocking the door without waking her was a bit of a trick, but I managed.

I had been in BJ's apartment before. It was a lot less cluttered than on my last visit. The furniture was the same. That was strange. Why hadn't the landlord gotten rid of everything before moving in a new tenant? Unless she was much closer to BJ than just an ex-lover. Was she a fiancé or wife? There were too many unanswered questions, and she was in no condition to talk.

I laid her down gently on top of the covers. Removing those strappy heels were a testament to my willpower, kneeling

down next to the bed, doing my best not to look up her dress. I held her foot against my chest, noticing how small her feet were compared to my hands. She blinked up at me from her back.
"What's going on?"
I grinned. "That depends on what you want."
She sucked in a breath, but her eyes rolled back in her head. I knew she had to be dizzy. What the hell had Ramón put in her drinks?
"I want out of my dress." She rolled onto her front. "It's hot in here."
I hesitated at the zipper. Did she know what she was asking? I had been with plenty of drunk women, but Mari didn't seem like the kind of girl that did this sort of thing. Why did I suddenly feel this need to protect her? Even from myself which was laughable. My libido usually ruled my life. I unzipped her dress slowly and untied the bow at the back. It felt like unwrapping a present. There was usually more participation going on at this stage in the evening. Mari laid there as still as can be. She must have fallen back asleep. I caressed her back, and she rolled her spine like a cat stretching. She moaned and rolled off the bed and started wiggling out of her dress.
"You're taking too damn long."
I smiled despite myself. She didn't have much patience.
The dress pooled around her feet and my mouth went dry. She was stunning, standing in nothing but a black thong. I didn't think it was possible, but the dress had actually hidden the extent of her figure. She was a skinny thing, but still had sexy curves.
"What's wrong with you?" Mari squinted at my face. "You should have your hands all over me by now."
She didn't have to tell me twice. I approached her and Mari melted into me, our bodies molding together as one. I slid my hands up her silky-smooth back, and ran my fingers through her long hair, tilting her head back for a kiss. She rested her palms on my chest, and her balance wobbled. Mari gripped my shirt and

# SANTA FE SEDUCTION

took over. The kiss was swift and brutal and had me groaning in seconds. She ground her body into mine, and then broke from the kiss.

"Did you know Benjie?"

Was she really going to do this now? What the hell? I didn't want to talk about her ex-lover, or whoever he was to her. He was dead. The last thing I needed was more guilt piled onto what I already felt. She must have realized her mistake when the silence ticked between us. Her lips found mine again and we got back on track. My mood was improving. I pushed her body to the mattress interested in nothing more than burying myself into her softness, killing a few hours. I needed an escape from the stress of the job, and I believed she needed this too. I planned to make her forget all about her ex-lover. She would be screaming my name, and after tonight that would be the only name coming from Mari's lips.

# SANTA FE SEDUCTION

## Chapter 6

*Mari*

Thump, Thump, Thump. I awoke to the sound of pounding. I blinked my eyes slowly looking around the room. Where was that noise coming from? Was that in my head? I groaned into my hands. My head was definitely throbbing, but that's not where the sound was coming from. It must be some neighbor exercising. It sounded mechanical. Maybe a rowing machine. I glanced at the clock. Seven in the morning. What the hell? I wanted to bang on all the apartment doors until I found the culprit and give him a piece of my mind. I don't know why I assumed it was a guy. I looked down and realized what I was wearing, which was nothing. Was the bartender still here? Maybe I could ask him to take care of the noise. I bet he would beat up the guy responsible. I had a vague recollection of the bartender bringing me home, but I couldn't remember much else after that. Had I gotten information about Benjie? I shook my head trying to clear my thoughts. That was a mistake. I ran to the bathroom and heaved. I hadn't gotten this drunk in years. What was in those drinks?

After downing a glass of water and pain killers, I went in search of clues around the apartment. My dress was in a pile on the floor. My shoes in another. My panties were hanging from the bedside lamp. The bedding was messed up. No notes, or any other signs that the bartender had been here. I realized I didn't even have Cruz's phone number. He had never given me his information at the drive-through or at the bar. Had we slept together, and I didn't even know his number or last name? Good one Mari. Geez. I guess it didn't matter if the bartender had spilled his guts about Benjie, since I couldn't seem to remember anything. I cringed at the thought of having to face everyone at the club again and go through the whole process again. I had a game plan last night, and had blown it bigtime, all because of a sexy Latin lover that literally danced my pants off. He had distracted me from my goals. I wasn't about to let him try it again, no matter what he said or did. If he had gotten some, I wasn't about to let that happen again. With mind made up, I went to search for Miles in the piles of clothes. He had probably been scared to death when I had come home drunk and out of my mind. I owed him a ton of cuddles and treats.

My outfit tonight was reserved. Well in comparison to last night. It was still sexy of course. A slinky black knee-length dress with V-neck and slits up the side. I wore it with black stiletto heels. It wasn't full on ho level slut-shaming. It was more ho adjacent. I arrived at the club and saw Cruz immediately. That man was built fine. I gave a little sigh watching the caramel-dipped eye candy polishing glasses and checking the stock levels of booze behind the bar. He flipped back his thick midnight hair. I desperately wanted to run my fingers through those unruly waves. Forget last night. Crank up the confidence. Regardless how little I remembered.

"You're back?"

I grinned. "Of course. I didn't get what I needed."

His eyebrows rose. "I thought I gave you exactly what you needed last night."

His deep voice sent shivers down my spine. I wanted so badly to ask what exactly he had given me, and would he do it

# SANTA FE SEDUCTION

again and again, until I couldn't see straight. I blew out a breath. Focus on the mission. Get answers.

Ramón bounced up behind the bar. "Ah. My tester is back. I'll make you up something special."

I shook my head. "As much as I'd love that. I'll have to pass. My tastebuds need a break."

Cruz smirked. Ramón's brow creased and he frowned. I'm not sure he could translate the word tastebuds. I'd let Cruz explain.

I glanced around and saw Rosa leaning against the far end of the bar and went to join her.

"Hey Rosa."

She smiled. "Did your plot pay off?"

"What plot was that?" I asked.

"The one that involved seduction."

I glanced at Cruz. At least he was out of ear shot. That would be embarrassing if he overheard our conversation. "I told you about that?"

"Yep. In the bathroom. You couldn't stop talking about it."

I groaned. "I can't remember a whole lot from yesterday."

"Yeah, my cousin Ramón was mixing your drinks. He's a Lorenzo. No wonder you can't remember."

"So, your family is filled with heavy drinkers?" I asked.

"Something like that."

She was being evasive, but I was hardly sharing everything myself. I guessed that Rosa had alcoholics in her family. I wasn't one to condemn for something like that. My stepdad had been one, and Benjie had been addicted to drugs.

"I guess we all have our addictions."

She tilted her head and squinted at me. It made me a little uncomfortable. Maybe I shouldn't have said that. It was obviously a sensitive subject. Maybe I could steer back to safer territory.

"All I have is vague recollections of the evening. I know Cruz took me home, and then he wasn't there this morning."

"It's probably for the best. One-night stands are meant to be forgotten."

"Why would you think it would just last one night?"

Rosa sighed. "You do know that Cruz doesn't date right? Didn't he give you the spiel?"

"Alcohol induced memory loss, remember?"

She chuckled. "Good point. Well, let me fill you in, 'cuz you seem alright, and I don't want to see you get hurt. Cruz is not a one-woman kind of guy. In the six months he's been working here, I've never seen him go home with the same woman twice. He is one of those bad boys. Trust me, bad boys are lots of fun, but I speak from experience, they are nothing but heartache. Cut your losses and move on."

That was disappointing. I had been debating if I should ask for a repeat performance. My head told me he was nothing but trouble, but my hormones had a mind of their own. Sounded like it wouldn't be an option anyhow. I decided to see if Rosa knew something about Benjie. There was plenty of other staff to question. Someone else might have remembered him.

"Do you remember a guy who worked here. He went by the name, BJ."

Rosa's eyebrows rose. "Are you a friend of his?"

I shrugged. "Something like that." I could be evasive too. Anyone who did recognize him and knew he died, tended to get weird when I told them he was my brother.

"He was a hard-working guy," She shrugged, "but he asked a lot of questions. Ramón took over his job two weeks ago. You know he died right?"

I nodded trying to keep the tears at bay.

"Listen, hon. You need to stop asking about him." Rosa whispered. She looked around the club like she was checking that

# SANTA FE SEDUCTION

no one was listening. "That guy was troubled. Not to mention there are eyes and ears everywhere."

Rosa left me at the edge of the bar even more confused than I was before. What did that mean? I thought it would be easy getting to the bottom of how he died. Why did no one want to talk about it? Maybe the cops had scared these people, or there was something more to this story. I needed hope that his death wasn't a simple suicide, or an accidental overdose. I knew in my heart that Benjie wouldn't have done it on purpose. From his last text message, he seemed upbeat. He had found a sense of purpose in life that had been missing for a long time. He was rectifying the wrongs from his past. Whatever that meant. The bottom line was he had gotten clean, and I believed him. I glanced at the other end of the bar. Cruz, Ramón, and Rosa were the only people here this early. Cruz must have sent Ramón to the back for more supplies. Was he the reason Rosa didn't want to talk about it? I decided to spend more time investigating Cruz, but from a distance. I choose a small booth close to the dance floor.

As the night drew on, I watched Cruz as he flirted with almost every woman in the bar. The guy was a total sleaze, not that any of the women he turned his gaze on seemed to mind. It was making me feel jealous even though I had no right to be. We had spent a single night together, and I didn't even remember it. Maybe I was getting more pissed that he barely even glanced in my direction.

"Would you like to dance?"

I blinked. A guy in a dark suit was standing by my booth. I hadn't even noticed his approach.

"Sure." I flipped my hair back, and he helped me out of the booth and onto the dance floor. This might be the perfect way to get Cruz out of my system. And it might give me the opportunity to track down people who knew Benjie.

"I know this sounds cliché but do you come here often?" I asked.

## ZIZI HART

The guy shook his head. "Nope. First time. But I like the scenery."

He was staring at my cleavage. Gag. And I thought Cruz was sleazy.

I smiled. I could pretend he was amusing for one dance.

When it was over, I couldn't get away from him quick enough.

Over the night, a few others asked for a dance, and a few more bought me drinks. I nursed two white wines. I wasn't about to make the same mistake from the previous night. The club wasn't quite as busy, since it was a Sunday. I wondered if I could get more answers during the week. I showed pictures of Benjie to anyone I could. A few had recognized him but couldn't give me much info. At the end of the night, I felt Cruz' eyes on me and turned toward the bar. His gaze met mine with intensity. Another man approached me, and Cruz' stare turned intimidating as hell. The drunk man didn't notice as he slid way too close to me in the booth.

"You looking for someone to take you home, sweetheart?"

I shook my head and swatted away the sweaty hand he rested on my knee. He smelled like he had bathed in Cuervo. How fitting. It was the club's signature scent. Typical drunk wouldn't take no for an answer and continued to hassle me. It reminded me of times working as a waitress in a Tempe bar. I looked around for the bouncer, to signal him over, but he was nowhere to be found. The only person paying any attention to the interaction was the last person I wanted help from, Cruz.

"Come on. I know you want what I've got."

I stuck my tongue out making my best yuck face, but it didn't seem to register.

The drunk grabbed my knee again, only this time he slid it higher on my thigh. He held on tight. A swat wasn't going to do the trick. I started to panic.

"Leave me alone."

# SANTA FE SEDUCTION

I tried to remember the self-defense course I had taken in college. I popped a quick knuckle to the throat and the guy started wheezing. He didn't leave, but at least he released his grip and I was able to climb over the table and get away. It wasn't graceful, but I didn't care at the moment. I bounced into Cruz' chest on my way out of the booth. He had made it over to my table in record time, and he wasn't even panting. His large frame seemed to swell in size as he stared at the drunk. Not that the guy was paying much attention. He was still catching his breath from my pop to his windpipe.

"You didn't need to intervene. I took care of things." I side-stepped Cruz and walked past him and hurried out of the club. Secretly, I was grateful that Cruz blocked the drunk's path, but I wasn't about to give him the satisfaction. Cruz was already far too cocky for his own good.

# Chapter 7

*Cruz*

I wanted to pummel the asshole that dared to grab her, but Mari had slipped out before things had escalated. She had flashed half the bar getting out of that booth. Those sexy dresses she wore were going to be the death of me. I had tried so hard not to watch her as man after man fondled her on the dance floor. I visualized punching them all. Rosa had noticed I was off tonight and kept asking if I was ok. I told her to blow me. She had bantered back something equally offensive, but I wasn't really paying attention. My focus was on one petite little firecracker that had managed to get under my skin. All she had to do was glance in my direction. An innocent blink of those long lashes, and I came undone. Every nerve ending on my body, felt like a live wire. It destroyed any hope at maintaining my normal calm reserve.

---

Over the next couple of days, Mari showed up at the club every night. It was driving me crazy. She kept asking questions, and I did what I could to dissuade her, but she didn't listen to me anymore. Well to be honest, I don't think she had ever listened to me to begin with, or anyone for that matter. Luckily Luís had his own problems and wasn't around often. And when he was there, he didn't pay much attention to the day-to-day affairs. It was her only saving grace. Only a few days had passed since Mari had gotten blackout drunk and I had driven her home. She hadn't asked me what happened that night, and I knew it must have been driving her nuts, the not knowing. Rosa had filled me in on their conversation. She had asked me if I had gotten anywhere with the girl. I had thrown my head back and laughed. I let my wicked gaze answer the question.

"You want the graphic details?"

Rosa sneered and walked away. I hadn't wanted to reveal the truth. Mari had undressed and thrown herself at me, but the grope fest had ended quickly when she passed out in bed. I had been noble leaving her untouched, snoring and snuggled under her covers. I had locked her apartment deadbolt with my spare key and slunk back to my own apartment sexually frustrated. Not that I would admit that to anyone. It was important everyone thought I was a womanizing asshole. My reputation was everything. The moment someone questioned my motives, was the day I would end up like BJ.

Mari had been more cautious with her alcohol consumption the last few days, sticking with a strict two-drink maximum. Men would buy her extra drinks, but she would refuse them outright or gift them to others. Not only did I see her at the club, we often ran into each other outside work as well. I couldn't seem to escape her intoxicating scent, or her scathing commentary.

Traveling down the produce aisle at the local grocery store, I noticed Mari searching through every bag of grapes. She was a little neurotic about finding the perfect bunch if you asked

# SANTA FE SEDUCTION

me. I don't know why I found it endearing instead of annoying. I snuck up behind her.

"They all get smooshed on the delivery truck."

She turned and growled.

"I didn't ask for your opinion."

"I'm here to serve, just the same." I grinned.

She shook her head and slipped the last bag she had been holding in her cart.

"Why are you following me?"

"Your ego must be huge. Can't I shop without you thinking it's some master plan to stalk you? I mean you're sexy in a thong, but I'm hit on every night at the club. It's not like I'm hurting for company."

Her mouth dropped. She sputtered and turned on her heels, heading to the other side of the store.

I smiled knowing I was a jerk, but not caring. She had it coming. I was pissed that she had given up on her plans to seduce me. I thought we could have had fun together. Maybe if I let her know that her plot had failed, it would encourage her to try again.

◆ — ◆ ⋖═◆═⋗ ◆ — ◆

Later that day at the Soap N' Suds, I had just put my last load of laundry in the dryer, when Mari walked in.

"You. Again."

My eyebrows rose. "I was here first chica. Maybe it's you who's stalking me."

Her head tilted and her mouth scrunched. "I'll give you that one."

I gave a double-take. Hmm. A concession? Was it possible that she was thinking logically for a change?

I watched her put several sexy underthings into a net bag trying not to imagine her wearing them. I failed. The silence stretched on as we both did our laundry. Most of our recent

## ZIZI HART

awkward encounters were filled with stifled conversation or uncomfortable silence. I was wondering if today would be any different. A stranger walked into the laundromat, and she pulled out a photo of BJ asking if they knew him. I shook my head. She had asked so many people from the neighborhood. Most people, including me, only knew him by his nickname, BJ. Mari really had it bad for him. I couldn't believe it, but I felt a hot streak of jealousy over the dead guy. Why did I care? So, what, if she still loved him? He was gone. Maybe it had more to do with the fact that she gave him more attention than me, and I wasn't used to that. I had never gotten jealous before. I kept wanting to tell her to leave it alone, but in the back of my mind, I knew it wouldn't matter. She was like a junk yard dog with a bone. Mari wasn't going to let it go, until you tore it from her dead corpse. That image sent shivers down my spine. How could I convey to her that was a real possibility? El Lobo Rojo was real, and he didn't live by society's rules. The guy was a psychopath, no matter how cleaned up he looked on the outside. The evil was still there. And no amount of detergent could ever clean the blood from his hands or the stains from his soul.

 The nights had been blending together the last six months and I felt like I was moving in a fog. The only light I had was when Mari would come to the club, like she was now. Tonight, she wore a spicy little green number, with gold heels. It would have looked ridiculous on almost anyone else but her. She never quite fit the scene. It was as if the world around her couldn't contain her vibrant energy.

 Rosa knocked on the bar. "Yo Cruz. Patrón for table 4."

 I blinked. How long had Rosa been standing there? I had been focused on Mari. It seemed to be my only pastime lately.

 I reached down to a hidden compartment underneath the bar and pulled out a special coaster and set a bottle of Patrón and 4 glasses on Rosa's tray. There was a system to business at the

# SANTA FE SEDUCTION

bar. I was one of the few who knew the inner workings. I needed to snap out of my current funk. What I really needed was to get laid, but ever since meeting Mari, I hadn't taken anyone else home. I hadn't been interested. I wondered if I was coming down with something. My shoulders shook and the shiver traveled down my spine.

"You want to go out tonight, Rosa?"

"Shut up Cruz." Rosa smiled as she said it. There was no heat to her words. It was more amusement than anything. I had been hitting on her for as long as I had worked here. But she still hadn't given in. It was probably for the best, being Luís' cousin and all. I'm not sure what I would have done if she had said yes. My heart wasn't really in it. Not that it typically mattered to my body. But lately the only one I dreamed of was Mari. She was the last thing I thought of when heading to bed, and the first thing on my mind when I woke. Maybe it had more to do with her innocence. That was an exotic commodity. Few people who frequented the club were innocent. I was as far from that as humanly possible. I had to get this obsession under control, because there was one thing I knew for certain. In my line of work, distractions got you killed.

# Chapter 8

*Mari*

The couple at the table in front of mine just ordered a bottle of Patrón. Not unusual. It seemed this club sold a lot of high-end specialty tequilas. The strange part was the chunky yellow quartz coaster it came on. Why would they put the alcohol on its own little gaudy pedestal? It seemed silly to me. But I had never worked at a high-end club, so what did I know? Maybe I was grasping at straws, trying to find meaning where there was none. I was obviously spending way too much time at the club. Maybe this journey was more about connecting with Benjie's past. I needed to find closure, but I started to wonder if I had made a mistake coming to Santa Fe. I should probably go back to Tempe and forget this whole trip. Why was I here? Was it guilt or simple curiosity? In the scheme of things, what did it really matter? Would answering the why change anything? He was still dead. Benjie wasn't coming back.

  I played with the straw in my drink, swirling it while scanning the club, lost in my thoughts. The girl who had gotten the Patrón looked around suspiciously and then slipped the coaster into her purse. What the hell? Why would she want to steal that gaudy thing? I might have missed it otherwise, but I had been looking in the perfect direction, and the dim lights had hit the crystal just right. Was the girl a klepto? Did I give a shit? Hadn't I just decided to give up? I sighed. It took me three whole seconds, before I raced to the bathroom to investigate. I was a step behind the woman. She paused at the counter watching me, but I dove into one of the stalls. The door had a large gap on the hinge side that I could peek through. I secretly watched as she opened up the bottom of the coaster. It held a few baggies filled with white powder. I assumed it was cocaine. I could feel the pulse in my throat as I stared at the woman. Was this normal? If so, how often had drugs been passed around in this manner? I had watched the delivery of drinks from the bar for the better part of the week, but I never remembered anything out of the ordinary. Other than the large, tacky coasters, I hadn't thought anything odd about the specialty cocktails or high-end bottle service. Most bars or clubs had a special way in how the high-end stuff was served. Some way to make it special, to make those getting it feel like the ridiculous price was somehow worth it. Bottles were served on fancy trays or in buckets of ice. Club Cuervo was no different.

Maybe it was a fluke. Perhaps Cruz didn't know anything about the drugs. It was possible. I desperately wanted to give him the benefit of the doubt, because despite his asshole ways, I still liked him. In that lust/hate sort of way. I decided to watch closer just to make sure. Now that I knew what to look for, I watched as more bottles were delivered around the club. That evening, I discovered a pattern. It was hardly a one-time occurrence. There was a sophisticated system in place, you just had to know what to look for. Cash was put into one of those leather check presenters. Plain black folders were sent for normal drink orders. Special folders with an embossed club's logo were sent with the high-end bottle service. The coasters carried the drugs. In every case, I saw the person remove baggies from the coaster.

Most were filled with white powder, but some had crystal or pills. Some customers were more subtle than others. The

# SANTA FE SEDUCTION

implications made my stomach clench. Cruz wasn't just involved. He was right smack dab in the middle of it. In fact, he looked to be running the show. I shook my head still not wanting to believe it, but I couldn't deny what I had seen with my own eyes. I was usually such a good judge of character and felt like Cruz was somehow a good guy, in a bad boy's bod, despite his rep with the ladies. I blew out a breath. More than likely Benjie had gotten his drugs from Cruz. If he had worked at the club for months, Benjie could have been selling the drugs as well. Or he could have refused. I had my suspicions on how Benjie OD'd. Accidental, my ass. It all made sense now, why Cruz hadn't wanted me to ask questions. It had been Cruz all along. He had been involved in everything, and I felt like a fool.

The real question was, what was I going to do with this information? Back in Tempe, I would have gone to the cops, but I didn't trust the cops in Santa Fe. They hadn't done a thing when Benjie overdosed. If he did in fact, overdose. That was still up for debate. I had talked to a lot of people here locally. Benjie had been making friends. He had been making decent money, and had sworn off drugs. That was the consistent message from his buddies. But had they known about the club? Maybe he had witnessed the deals and said something? I couldn't see my brother involved in selling the stuff. Maybe it was just a sister's naïve hope that her brother hadn't done something so spectacularly stupid. I watched as Cruz gave one of his patented glares to a customer. There must have been a dispute over the price. Cruz was spinning the coaster like a top on the bar. He slapped his hand down and the coaster stopped. Two goons appeared behind the customer and dragged him away. I gulped. Cruz wasn't just the dealer; he had enforcers too.

Benjie could have been killed because he saw too much. Suddenly my trip to Santa Fe took on a whole new dynamic. Maybe I should be listening to all those insisting I stop asking questions. There had been whispers of a name, El Lobo Rojo. I think it meant the Red Wolf in Spanish. People said the Red Wolf had a way of dealing with troublemakers. I could be next on the list of those to be silenced. Like I had summoned his awareness, Cruz stared in my direction. I didn't want his attention, damn it. Especially not now. I polished off my glass of wine, left a tip, and got the eff out of there.

The cool breeze hit me when I stepped outside the club. It had been hot inside with all the bodies, but it wasn't refreshing. I suddenly felt cold inside. I shivered. Cruz had been to my apartment when I was unconscious. He had seen me naked. We might have been together in the biblical sense. What if he had Benjie killed? I started feeling queasy. I had to get out of here. I looked in my rearview mirror the whole way back to my apartment. I felt like I was being followed, but I couldn't be sure. I sprinted up the rickety stairway nearly breaking a leg in my heels. My hands were shaking so badly, I could barely get the key in the lock. When I finally managed to get inside, I slammed and bolted the door and sagged down onto the floor with a sigh of relief. My pulse was in my throat, heart pounding. Miles was there by my side. Butting his head against my hand. I picked him up grateful for the comfort. I glanced back at the door. It didn't look all that sturdy, but I didn't have much of a choice. I couldn't afford a hotel. I moved a chair under the doorknob and climbed into bed.

It took me forever to fall asleep, and once I did, I had nothing but nightmares. I tossed and turned. My dreams had Cruz coming into my apartment. He stared at me while I slept. I wasn't sure if it was memories from our drunken night together, or if it was just my paranoia manifesting itself in my dreams. Regardless, it freaked me out. He could have easily done something to me that night. Cruz knew where I lived. He had driven me home. I thought about all the things I discovered at the club. I was scared to go back, wondering what else I would witness, and how much danger I was really in.

# Chapter 9

*Mari*

The next morning, I woke up exhausted. I was grateful to have made plans for the day. I needed to get out of the apartment. I had an appointment with Benjie's counselor at the rehab center. After getting a list of numbers from my brother's phone bill, I had plenty of people to question. I was hoping to visit a few of his closest friends while I was there. When pulling into the parking lot of the center, I noticed a local News crew setting up, so I stopped by to see what they were doing. A philanthropist was going to donate money to the center.

I went into the brown brick building and found Suite 101. The office didn't look like much. It definitely wasn't one of those fancy Beverly Hills places for the rich and famous. This one looked more like a government facility, with cheap plastic seats and laminate desks. The receptionist was smiling at an attractive older gentleman in an expensive business suit sitting in the waiting area flipping through a magazine. I waited a few minutes before she turned in my direction. In fact, I had to clear my throat twice to get her attention.

"Sorry about that." Her cheeks went pink.

"I'm here to see Counselor Joy at 10 o'clock."

"Oh. I'm sorry. She's going to be running a bit late for your meeting. I'm not sure if you noticed out front, but there's a news crew here. Mr. Lorenzo over there is going to be donating a hefty check to our Rehab clinic." She gave him a dazzling smile. The receptionist was frumpy with wrinkles around her tired eyes, but she appeared to be flirting with him. He looked up and returned her smile. She sighed.

"He is such a wonderful man. We do get federal and state grants, but it's really the private donors that keep the doors open. Mr. Lorenzo is an absolute saint."

He chuckled to himself as he flipped through another magazine. I wasn't sure if he was paying attention to our conversation, or just embarrassed by the accolades.

Since it seemed like I would be waiting for a bit, I took a seat and struck up a conversation with the man.

"Hello Mr. Lorenzo. I'm Mari."

"Have we met?"

I shook my head. "I would have remembered."

"What brings you here?"

"My brother."

"Is he here at the center?"

I shook my head. "No. He died from an overdose."

"I'm so sorry for your loss." He reached out and palmed my hand. "You poor dear."

His eyes held such feeling of remorse. I wasn't used to a lot of eye contact, or touching for that matter. My family had never been overly affectionate. Hugs were rare. The whole situation made me a little uncomfortable and I looked away. He patted my hand. The gesture might have been calming for most people, but to me it felt strange. I wondered briefly if he had ever worked in therapy. He would have been good at it. Guessing from the suit, I guessed his profession to be quite the opposite.

"I had a family member that went the same way. I understand how hard it is. Sometimes you feel better when you

# SANTA FE SEDUCTION

talk about it?" He said it like a question. Open ended. He seemed genuinely concerned.

I realized that I hadn't really talked about it with anyone, including my friends back in Tempe. Most of them had grown up quite differently. They hadn't been abused, or had to deal with drug addictions and death at such a young age. I don't know why I felt the need to keep myself closed off. I hadn't invited anyone to the funeral. It had taken place in Santa Fe. There was no family left that we talked to, and since I hadn't known who Benjie's local friends were at the time, I had no one to notify. He had burned a lot of bridges over the years including one with me. We had fought when he moved out and left me with our abusive step-dad. It had taken me years to forgive him for that. We had a strained relationship, but over the last year, had made progress mending the bridge. We texted back and forth fairly regularly. It had been mostly superficial stuff. Nothing that really gave me a clue about his life, other than the basics. My friends would have never understood my relationship with my brother. It would be nice to finally talk about it with someone who understood. This kind man had experienced something similar. Would it be so bad to open up to some stranger? I'd probably never run into him again. From his designer shoes and fancy suit, it was certain we didn't run in the same circles.

"Do you live in Santa Fe?"

"No. I'm from Tempe, Arizona. I'm just visiting. You know getting stuff in order."

"I take it your brother had treatment here at one time."

"Yeah. He's seen Counselor Joy for a few years. I guess I'm mostly here for closure."

"That is important. You can't move on until that happens. I remember wanting to make sense of it all when my cousin died. But my dear, realize that not everything can be explained, especially where addicts are concerned. Sometimes they don't make rational decisions. Behaviors are erratic, and illogical. Their world is chaos, and they tend to react badly when things go wrong."

"You're probably right. I doubt I'm going to get the answers I'm hoping for. In the back of my brain, I realize that. But I also can't bear to do nothing. My guilt won't allow it."

"I get that. Believe it or not, I got into fist fights long ago after my cousin died. Actions allow us to focus on the physical, so we can repress what we feel."

I smiled. I couldn't picture this polished man doing anything like that. It just didn't fit. I could barely imagine him throwing a punch, let alone getting dirt or blood on his perfectly pressed suit. The idea of him getting into a brawl was laughable.

His eyes crinkled and he grinned. "These days, this is my Call to Action. I can't see a more vital cause than to keep drugs off the streets and help those with addictions, recover. It's a way to remember my cousin. That's my way of coping with the loss."

The receptionist called Mr. Lorenzo, and he went into the office with a nod. After about fifteen minutes, he and a woman, I assumed to be Counselor Joy exited and walked out the front door to where the cameras were set up. I watched through the window as the reporter went through a series of questions, and Mr. Lorenzo handed one of those obnoxiously large checks to Counselor Joy.

It took another half hour for them to finish up before I was escorted into Joy's office.

"Thank you so much for meeting me. I didn't realize how busy it would be."

She smiled. "It's a great reason to run late. It means more funding to help more people. But I'm still sorry you had to wait."

Now that I was in her office, I couldn't remember a single one of the huge list of questions I had wanted to ask her. Wasn't that always the case? Maybe all I really wanted was to see how others felt about him at the end. I hoped that would give me some sense of what he was going through.

# SANTA FE SEDUCTION

"What do you remember about Benjie?"

"He went by BJ here. He used to love telling raunchy jokes about it too. He had quite the sense of humor, at least when he was in good spirits. He was a great guy and worked hard at beating his addiction. I thought he had finally overcome it. A lot of them say they do, but BJ seemed to have turned his life around. He had a steady job, and was going to regular support group meetings. I thought for sure it would stick this time. It was a huge shock when I found out he had overdosed."

"Why is that?"

"There were no signs of a relapse. No triggers. He wasn't shaky or uncertain. No missed appointments or meetings. You usually see people withdraw first. The last time I had seen him, he was in a great mood. He mentioned wanting to make amends for all the wrongs he had done in his life. BJ had a purpose, and a passion. He shared more in group sessions and seemed genuinely happy. I just didn't understand when the call came in. It didn't make any sense."

"That's how I felt too. Whenever he called or texted me, it felt different too. I've been through so many years when he would get clean, and then relapse. But for the first time, it felt different. I could tell he had hope for the future."

"That's why it was so bizarre." Joy shook her head. "A week before his death, we were talking in group about how he wanted to celebrate his one-year sobriety. Since most of the addicts don't drink because that's a trigger, a bar was out. And since a restaurant might be too expensive, he didn't want any friends excluded that couldn't afford it, so he had come up with a different idea."

Joy pulled out a printed invitation from a desk drawer and handed it to me.

"BJ made these on the computer at the library. He had decided to do a potluck picnic at the park. He was inviting all his friends from the center. BJ even spent his own money getting dozens of hamburgers and hot dogs to grill. In fact, we still have them stored in the clinic's freezers."

"Thanks for sharing all that with me." I nodded gratefully. I'm glad I wasn't the only one confused by his death. She handed me a tissue and took one for herself, drying her tears.

"Such a wonderful kid." Joy sniffed. "We have a grief counseling session tonight. Family and friends are welcome. I'd love for you to come."

I wasn't sure I really wanted to, but I didn't know how to tell her no.

"Some of BJ's friends might show up. He made quite a few in rehab."

That didn't surprise me. Benjie had always made friends easy. He had since we were little. There was just something about him. I decided it was another opportunity to talk to more people. If more people thought the circumstances of his death were strange, maybe my suspicions were correct.

"What time is the session?"

"Six o'clock."

"I should be able to."

"Are any of Benjie's friends at the clinic now?"

"One. Normally we aren't supposed to invite outsiders to talk to them while they are going through detox. There are privacy issues, but the biggest reason is that oftentimes friends and family are triggers. Their reason behind why they continue to relapse. But in this case, I believe it might help you both heal."

Joy got up and escorted me through a series of doors toward the middle of the building.

"Who will I be meeting?"

"Federico. BJ's sponsor. He's regressed. BJ's death hit him hard."

## SANTA FE SEDUCTION

  Federico was a short Spanish fellow, maybe in his late thirties.
  He gave a half grin when I approached.
  "You BJ's sister?"
  I nodded.
  "I see the resemblance."
  I grinned. "Most people don't notice."
  "You have the same nose and chin."
  "From our mother. We have different dads."
  "Full or half-sister. It don't matter. Family is family."
  I liked that.
  "I still don't understand." Federico shook his head. "BJ had sworn off drugs for good. His commitment was solid. No wavering. He had purpose. When I found him lying on the floor in his apartment, I snapped." His eyes turned glassy. Federico sniffed and wiped his eyes with a sleeve.
  "If he couldn't make it, why didn't he reach out to me?" His shoulders slumped. "I don't know. I guess I just gave up after that. I wanted to escape from reality, so I did." He laughed. "BJ would have been so pissed at me. But then again, maybe not. He slid too. Maybe I just wanted to join him."
  "Was he dating anyone? Maybe a girl broke his heart?" I asked.
  "Not anyone he told me about."
  "The whole thing doesn't make sense."
  He nodded. "BJ was a good friend. We told each other everything."
  "He was a good brother too. Even though half the time, I wanted to smack him."
  We spent the rest of the time telling stories and making each other laugh. BJ had seemed similar to how I remembered him from high school. Full of energy and humor and hope. I agreed that it didn't make sense for him to jump from hope to despair in a matter of days. Federico had only lost contact with

him for two days. That's why he had gone to his apartment to check on him. That's where he had found him. Federico had been the one to call the police.

---

It was six o'clock and I was sitting on a cheap plastic chair with a group of strangers, wondering why I had agreed to come. It was sure to dredge up memories I would rather leave buried. But I was looking for closure, and this had a chance of offering me some. Being surrounded by others going through something similar made me feel like I wasn't alone. And I had felt alone most of my life. The chairs were arranged in a circle in a small room with worn carpet and peeling wall paper. I nodded to Luís who was sitting on the other side of the circle next to Counselor Joy. Odd that he was here, but at least I did know two people, so they weren't all complete strangers. Although I had only just met those two this morning, and I didn't form friendships like Benjie did. Maybe I should try to be more like my brother had been and give this group a chance. I took a deep breath and let it out slow, wondering if anyone else was as nervous as I was. We all went around and introduced ourselves and shared why we were there.

"My name is Mari."

"Hi Mari." Everyone in the group responded.

It was a little unnerving being the center of attention.

"My brother Benjie died from an overdose. I don't really know why I'm here. I guess I'm looking for answers. Asking the big question. Why? Why did he do it? Why couldn't he stop using? Why am I so angry at him? I blame him for his weakness, then I feel guilty. Why am I such a lousy sister? I wonder if there is something I could have done. Maybe I could have called a little more. Sympathized. Understood better. Yelled less. I guess I just want things to make sense."

Several in the group nodded.

# SANTA FE SEDUCTION

"Same here." One woman stated.
"I'm with you." A teen agreed.
"That was a great share." Counselor Joy smiled at me.

I don't know why but it made me feel a little lighter getting all that off my chest. No one had said it was stupid to blame myself or feel guilty. A few others offered similar sentiments as they shared stories of loved ones that had passed. Luís Lorenzo shared such a heart-felt story about his cousin, that everyone in the group shed tears. He was such an amazing speaker. It was his mission in life to do everything he could to help those with addiction. I had never met someone so passionate. I wished that Benjie had a role model like him when he had grown up. Perhaps then, his life would have turned out differently. After the group broke for the evening, and we had stacked all the chairs, Joy called me over to meet a few boys that had showed up late. They were some of Benjie's friends that wanted to share their condolences.

"I'm so sorry for your loss. I really thought BJ had it beat."
"Man, he fooled me."
"Did BJ ever talk about a girl?" I asked.
"Nah., He wanted to be clean for a year before getting serious."
"He may have met someone at the club he worked at." One of the kids offered. "There are tons of hot chicks at the club."
"Did you guys go to the club?"
"Oh hell no. Bars are off limits." The guy grinned at Joy. "Right doc?"
"Whatever works. If avoiding those places helps you, then stick with it."
"I was stunned when I first learned that Benjie worked in a bar. Maybe that's how he slipped."
The other kid shrugged. "Maybe."
"Did you ever meet any of his work friends from the bar?"
"He kept that part of his life separate." Joy answered. "He said it was to keep the evil influences away from those struggling

to get clean. But maybe that had been part of the problem. He hadn't listened to his own advice." She shrugged. "I wish I could give you more," Joy sighed. "But often times we never the get answers we seek."

---

After dinner and snuggles with Miles, I crawled into bed thinking of all I had learned at the rehab center. Maybe Joy was right. If his Counselor and closest friends couldn't find a reason, what chance did I have, his estranged sister? He had lived on his own for eight years. Seven of those we barely had any contact. I hated to admit it, but I didn't really know him anymore. In my head, I kept picturing Benjie when we were both younger, before life had taken its toll. I had looked up to my big brother back then. He seemed to know everything. I remembered times when I would get upset, and he would tell me jokes to cheer me up. One right after another just like a standup comedian. I would be rolling with laughter for hours. Humor got us through those tough times after our mother had died. I couldn't give up. Maybe it was pointless, but I didn't care. I wasn't going to stop searching for answers. Benjie deserved nothing less.

# Chapter 10

*Mari*

The next morning, bleary eyed from a restless sleep, I poured myself a bowl of cereal and plopped onto the couch and flipped on the remote. Miles joined me. He climbed up my shirt and stuck his paw into the bowl of milk daring me to complain. I lifted an eyebrow and sighed. He was testing me. I took a big bite of cereal and glared at the kitten. I was hungry and didn't feel like sharing my food this morning. He wasn't put off by my attitude. Miles hopped off my lap and settled into one of the cushions watching me finish eating. I thought I might let him lick the bowl if he was good.

Luís Lorenzo was on the morning news. The name roused my interest, and I turned up the volume. He was talking to the reporter about his work with under-privileged children, giving back to the community, and doing charity work around the city. He mentioned his donation to the rehab center and praised the work that Counselor Joy and others at the facility were doing. He handed Joy a giant check and I realized it was the same thing I had witnessed the day before through the office window. It must have been taped. I hadn't heard what had been said at the time. He was truly an eloquent speaker with loads of charisma. The reporter repeatedly blushed when he smiled at her.

Luís told a story of how he came to this country and because of his work ethics and family values, built a business from the ground up. He had succeeded in the American Dream. Luís Lorenzo was a model citizen, and a powerful businessman in the Santa Fe community. He talked about several of the business enterprises he had launched within Santa Fe, but the shocker was his ownership of Club Cuervo. He was having a special fund raiser this evening. I had been debating what to do with the information I had discovered at the club regarding the drug deals. I now knew what I had to do. I would go and see Luís this evening. He had invited everyone from the neighborhood. They were having specials, and all the proceeds would go to charity. If I could get him alone, I might be able to fill him in on what was happening at his own club. If I could get the drug trade to stop, maybe I would feel better somehow. I owed it to Benjie, to at least try.

I went to the club early, like usual, but the place was already packed. There were reporters and cameras taking shots of Luís in front of his club. His kitchen staff stood behind him. The reporter talked about all the ethnic dishes his club boasted, and Cruz was there to talk about all the drink specials. The media specialist, an attractive Hispanic woman talked about all the events, including dance competitions and charity galas that would be happening later that year.

I made a point to catch Luís' eye and asked if I might have a private moment to discuss something of a personal nature. With eyebrows raised, he agreed to meet me in the VIP lounge later in the evening. I wasn't sure exactly what he expected. Afterwards, I thought it might have sounded like I was hitting on him. I hoped he didn't think that was the case, that would make what I had to

# SANTA FE SEDUCTION

discuss with him even more embarrassing. Luís was probably 30 years my senior. In my mind that qualified as far too old. He was probably my dad's age if he had still been alive. That was just plain creepy.

At around eleven, one of Mr. Lorenzo's associates escorted me from the VIP room to his office where we could have our discussion in private.

"I wanted to make it clear I wasn't hitting on you earlier." I blushed.

I was really sticking my foot in my mouth.

"I mean, I didn't want you to think," I stammered. "Well, you know."

He shook his head and laughed.

"I understand completely. You had me intrigued by all the mystery. My curiosity is what really got me. Please." He gestured to the couch. "Take a seat. Tell me what is on your mind."

I blew out a breath and plopped in the cushy leather couch. Now that I was here, I hesitated. What if he thought I was nuts. A conspiracy theorist. Or worse yet, if he thought I was blaming him.

"First let me begin by saying how much I admire you. For all the work you have done with charity. It's so inspiring."

"Thank you." He grinned. "I'm blessed and grateful I have the opportunity to give back." His eyes twinkled.

"I don't want you to think for a moment I blame you for what is happening in your club. I want you to be aware, so you can take the necessary action."

"You have my undivided attention my dear."

"I've noticed some things. With the coasters at the bar. Your bartender is selling drugs."

"Cruz Diaz?"

I nodded.

"I can't believe that. Are you sure?"

"Yeah. I'm sure. I've witnessed it multiple times. I saw drugs in baggies come out of the coasters, and money go into special folders. Cruz is involved in the entire process."

I took a deep breath. "But that's not all. He could be doing more than that."

"Do tell." He folded his hands flat in a prayer position tapping his fingers to his lips.

"I believe he had something to do with my brother's murder."

I started tearing up and he pulled out a few tissues and handed them to me.

"My brother's name is Benjie Jones, but most people called him BJ. He worked as a barback for Cruz. I think he might have seen too much and Cruz might have had him killed. The cops say Benjie overdosed, but I know my brother and he swore off drugs a year ago after completing rehab. All his friends said he was clean. He had gotten rid of everything. There was no drug paraphernalia in his apartment. It doesn't make sense."

A tick twitched on his cheek and he leaned toward me, his hands clenching his knees. His reaction was a little unnerving, but I knew it was a lot to take in. I still hadn't processed it fully. I'm sure it was triggering some of the same questions he experienced when his cousin died. Or maybe it was just the fact that an employee had been selling drugs under his nose. That had to be difficult to fathom considering how much of an advocate he was for saving those with addictions.

Luís sat there in silence for a few minutes. He got up from his seat and went over to some monitors at the far side of the room. He whispered a few things into an ear piece I didn't realize he had been wearing until just then.

"We are going to fix everything my dear. I bet you could use a stiff drink. I know I could." He went over to the small bar area and poured two glasses of whiskey from a decanter.

# SANTA FE SEDUCTION

I leaned back into the couch letting my head fall back and closed my eyes. Now that I had gotten it all out, I was relieved. It hadn't exactly given me closure, but deep down, I wasn't sure I really expected it to.

Luís appeared behind the couch and leaned over handing me a thick glass tumbler. Amber liquid sloshed around and I wondered if I should refuse. I never drank whiskey straight before.

He walked around the couch and held up his glass speaking words in Spanish. I had taken Spanish in high school and knew plenty of words, but the phrase eluded me. It was clearly some sort of toast, but I had no idea of the meaning. Luís tilted his head, when I didn't lift the glass to my lips. He was clearly expecting me to drink. The last thing I wanted to do was offend him, after he was willing to believe my story. I took a long swig. It went down a lot smoother than I thought it would, but it was still stronger than what I was used to.

"What did those words mean?" I wheezed.

"It's a Lorenzo family toast." He chuckled. "It loses a little on the translation, but roughly means. To Revenge. It should always be served neat."

That sounded ominous. But to be fair, I hadn't really started this journey only looking for information. If I was honest with myself, what I really wanted was retribution. I lifted my glass, "To justice."

He had a strange expression I couldn't quite place, but he nodded and polished off his drink and placed the glass on the coffee table. I took a sip this time. The last thing I wanted to do was get tipsy.

Luís grabbed a pen and paper and started asking more questions about what I had seen. After about 20 minutes, he seemed to run out of things to ask. I felt like that was my queue to leave. He could resolve this matter without me. As an important businessman, he wouldn't get the runaround from the police like I had. Luís agreed to keep me in the loop on what he discovered.

# ZIZI HART

I was getting a little sleepy from the whisky and figured I better make my way home before exhaustion overwhelmed me. I tried to get up, but my legs weren't cooperating. "Um. Luís. I'm having some issues here." I felt like a fool. Drunk after a couple of sips of alcohol. He was going to think I was a total lightweight. I was embarrassed as all hell, but I needed his help, or I was never getting out of his office. "Would you mind calling me a cab?"

Luís grinned, but it wasn't soothing. It was a sinister gnashing of teeth, nothing like what he presented to the media cameras earlier in the evening.

"Why should I do that, my dear?"

My head was getting really heavy. It took effort to keep it pointing in the direction of his voice. It suddenly lolled to the right. Luís came around to look me in the eye since I seemed to have lost the ability to hold my head upright. He no longer had the expression of concern he had given me a half hour before. That mask was long gone. I tried to scream, but words could no longer form in my throat. It came out as an incoherent jumble of vowels. Just before I passed out, he whispered something to me in Spanish that made my pulse thunder in my throat. I realized too late, that I had made a horrible mistake.

# Chapter 11

*Cruz*

The club was insane tonight, but it was finally starting to calm down. I hadn't taken a break for hours. I cracked my neck and glanced at my watch. Ramón still had tons of energy. We had both been serving drinks. At least he was getting a lot of experience.

I shook my head at his enthusiasm. He should have been dead on his feet like I was, but the kid was like the Energizer bunny.

Rosa emerged from the crowd. She was making her way over to the bar. At least she was frazzled and exhausted. I wasn't the only one.

"You're exactly who I wanted to see." She panted. Rosa planted a kiss on my lips before I realized what she was doing, molding her body into mine. I lost all train of thought. Ramón whistled behind me.

"I need you, Cruz." She whispered in my ear.

I blinked. My brain was still foggy. Where had this come from? I had been hitting on her for months, but had pretty much written her off. It was clear she wasn't interested. What had changed her mind?

## ZIZI HART

A range of emotions hit me, and I realized that my interest had faded. I had continued to ask Rosa out because the banter between us was routine, but I didn't really desire her anymore. To be honest, the only one I had really been attracted to since working here had been Mari. She was so different from the women I dated, if you could call what I did dating. Mari seemed to be untouched by the seedy elements that surrounded me on a daily basis. I couldn't believe it, but I was going to do the unthinkable and tell Rosa I wasn't interested. I valued her friendship more than anything, and even though I knew I wouldn't be here for much longer. I didn't want to give up a friendly face, no matter how short the time. Rosa put a finger to my lips, as if she could see the refusal in my eyes. There was something in hers, a spark, but it wasn't sexual. It radiated urgency. I knew something was wrong, but she obviously wouldn't or couldn't speak of it in public. Since Rosa was usually blunt to a fault, that made me realize just how serious the situation was. I had to get her somewhere private so we could talk.

"Hey Ramón. I thought I would leave early tonight." I watched Rosa's reaction. She nodded her head. We were on the same page. "Would you be ok closing up?"

"Sure thing." He grinned. "I close up. No problem."

"Thanks man. I appreciate it."

I walked out the back with Rosa curled into my side. I was hoping when we were alone, she would explain what was going on. To anyone watching, it seemed like she was flirting, but I had watched her with others at the club, and I knew she was feigning interest. Every movement she made was filled with tension. She was really worried about something.

"We need to stop in the storage closet and grab my roller bag." She whispered in my ear.

I nodded. I'd go along with the charade.

There were two goons standing in front of Luís' office. Rosa started kissing me.

# SANTA FE SEDUCTION

"Make it look good for Frick & Frack." She whispered into my ear.

I grinned. We were putting on a show. I could do that. I shoved her against the wall and kissed her hard, the line of my body pressing into hers. Rosa grunted at the impact, and hesitated for only a moment, before responding in force. She shoved me back to the other wall in the hallway and opened the door to the storage closet. She slammed the door behind us when we were inside. I heard José and Bruno chuckle. Inside the closet, she ripped my shirt, popping a few buttons in the process. Her hands were everywhere, but it wasn't seductive. She pulled out the lipstick from her purse and slathered it on and started kissing me on my lips, neck, cheek and chest, anyplace that was visible. It had taken me by such surprise, that I stumbled back into the shelves knocking stuff over, causing supplies to clatter to the floor. Thank goodness there wasn't much back here that was breakable, but it made a terrible racket. She held up a finger for me to keep silent. Rosa messed up her own hair and clothes. We both looked properly debauched. She extended the handle to a large roller bag and motioned for me to grab it.

"This bag isn't heavy." She patted my arm and whispered. "Sell it."

What the hell was I getting into?

As soon as we left the closet, Rosa tried to fix her clothes, but she seemed to be flashing more skin in the process. The goons focused all their attention on her, which I believe was her intention.

"Gentlemen, I'm leaving early tonight with Cruz. Ramón is tending bar."

One of the goons noticed the bag. "What's in there?"

"It's my clothes and stuff for my trip back home tomorrow, and it's none of your damn business."

She shoved me out the back door and I heard snickering behind us. The bag was heavy as hell, but I made it look like it was nothing. At least it was on wheels. She signaled for me to put the bag in her car. "I'll follow you to your apartment."

"What's this all about it?"

"Not here." She looked up at one of the security cameras I knew that Luís had up around the property. She gave me another passionate kiss, but I knew it was only for show.

Ten minutes later we pulled into the apartment parking lot. I still didn't have a clue what Rosa was doing. She parked next to me and opened the trunk.

"I don't know how far my cousin's reach goes. Don't react." Rosa fully unzipped the bag, and I realized there was a dead body inside. It was a small-boned woman with long dark hair covering her face. I had to stop this. I couldn't be implicated in a murder.

"I won't be a part of this."

"It's Mari. She was in trouble."

I glanced at her still form. No. She couldn't be dead. My chest tightened and my stomach plummeted. I studied her torso and detected a slight rise and fall of her chest. Mari was clearly unconscious. Not murdered. My breath whooshed out of me. That was good, but that meant I was now part of a kidnapping. Not a whole lot better, but I'd take it.

"Come on. We need to get into your apartment and out of sight." She zipped up the bag and gestured for me to pick it up.

Rosa went into the back seat and grabbed several bags under a blanket that looked to be filled with clothes and shoes. She carried them up to my apartment. We walked in silence until I unlocked the door.

"Drugs?" I asked.

"Yeah. She was drugged. Mari was like this when I found her."

# SANTA FE SEDUCTION

When we were inside the apartment with the door bolted, she unzipped the bag, and Mari's body tumbled out. I carried her to the couch and covered her with a blanket.

"There's a secret sliding door that goes from Luís' office to the storage closet. I was in there when Luís was talking to Mari. After he left, I dragged her to the closet. My bag was already in there. I just had to move some of my clothes so she would fit."

I ran a hand through my hair. "I warned her."

"So did I. She asked too many questions about BJ. And Luís found out. I heard Frick and Frack talking about it. You know what Luís was going to do to her." She shook her head. "I had no choice but to intervene. I'm not going to be a part of another senseless death."

My eyes widened. Did that mean my suspicions were accurate? Had Luís killed BJ? And had Rosa witnessed it?

# Chapter 12

### Mari

Whispered words reached my ears and I slowly blinked, taking in unfamiliar surroundings. The couch I was sprawled across was soft and cozy, just like the blanket that was wrapped around me. It was nothing like the stiff leather couch from Luís' office. My eyes flew open. How did I get here? I remembered talking with Luís, doing a few toasts. Then my vision had blurred, and my limbs had turned to jelly. I had been completely immobile when Luís had whispered words I would never forget. He had stated in no uncertain terms that I would soon be joining my brother. I had to get out of here.

The voices started coming closer. And as desperate as I was to see who it was, I forced myself to close my eyes and try to remain as still as possible, hoping they would think I was still unconscious. It wasn't much, but it was the only advantage I had. After just a few words, I recognized their voices. It was Cruz and Rosa. Had they kidnapped me? Was the whole staff involved with the drug deals? I was so stupid not to realize that everyone was in on it. Mari, you're an idiot, I chastised myself. I remembered that Rosa was usually the one to deliver the special coasters to the guests. I had witnessed it, but it hadn't registered in my thick skull. I had justified her actions. She was a waitress. It was her job to deliver drinks. I assumed that Rosa had been oblivious to the drug deals. Because we had formed a friendship of sorts, I couldn't see the situation clearly.

It had been that way with Benjie too. I never realized he had a drug problem. He was just going through hard times, but he would work out his issues, and be back to his normal self in no time. Look how that turned out. I've been so fucking naïve. I could just kick myself. I should have realized more people needed to be involved to make this sort of thing work. Just how big was this operation? Was Luís the one in charge? That would make sense, he was the owner of the club after all. Of course, he knew what was happening. My brain was still processing everything, but I had to sort through all the facts so I could devise a plan to get out of this situation. I refused to be another casualty, like my brother. Luís had spiked my drink. He intended to kill me. Everyone at the club was more than likely involved in drug trafficking or worse. The cops were either incompetent, or involved as well. Was I just being paranoid, or did everyone seem like a suspect?

I heard a phone buzz.

"Luís just texted." Rosa stated.

"What did he say?"

"Where the fuck are you, ho-bag?"

"Your cousin talks to you like that?"

"Actually, that's tame for him. He must have heard from Frick and Frack that we walked out together."

Several seconds of silence made me want to blink my eyes open, but I remained still.

"What did you type back?" Cruz asked.

"I'm getting laid, and he should mind his own fucking business."

Cruz chuckled.

# SANTA FE SEDUCTION

What the Fuck? These two were hooking up when I was out cold. Forget the drug deals and the kidnapping. I no longer gave a shit if they knew I was awake. I opened my eyes and sat up, or at least tried to. It would have been more dramatic if I hadn't have gotten twisted up in the blankets. They jumped. At least I had the satisfaction of surprising them.

Rosa was the first to compose herself. "Good. You're awake. We've got questions and not a lot of time."

I stared at them, standing next to one another. Their clothes were rumpled. There were rips and buttons missing. They both had bedhead, and Rosa's lipstick was smeared across Cruz's neck and face. It was pretty evident they had just finished ravaging each other not that long ago. I knew Cruz had been hitting on Rosa, but I had no idea they had sealed the deal. Jealousy heated me from the inside out. I wasn't really focusing on the big picture. He was the bad guy. A drug dealer. I shouldn't care who he slept with.

Cruz snapped his fingers in front of my face. I slapped them away. "What are you doing?"

He shrugged. "Your eyes glazed over. I thought maybe the drugs were kicking in again."

"Did you drug me?"

"What? No. Of course not. Why would you think that?"

Rosa sat next to me and patted my leg. "It was Luís. He put something in your drink. I overheard your conversation with him and told Cruz. We got you out of there." She shook her head. "You should be thanking us."

They were saying the right things, but I still didn't trust them.

"Isn't Luís family?"

"Don't remind me." She rolled her eyes. "We may share the same last name and be related by blood, but I'm nothing like my cousin."

I wasn't sure what to believe. My head was pounding. I rubbed my temples.

"Look. I don't want to press you, but we don't have any time to delay. Is there anything you need from your place? Luís will be sending someone over there to look for you. Think of anything he can use as leverage."

"Miles!" I screeched. "I need to get Miles."

"You have a son?" Cruz asked.

"What? No, he's a kitten. I rescued him. Luís wouldn't hurt him, would he?"

They both looked at one another, expressions grave.

Cruz left to go make a phone call in the bedroom. Rosa asked me if I needed some water, aspirin, or another blanket. I didn't want to accept her help, and I definitely didn't want to sit here and wait. I needed to do something, but first I needed answers.

"Where are we?"

Rosa rattled off the cross streets.

"That's my complex, Viejo Sol Station."

She shook her head. "We're next door at Luna Nueva Apartments."

Cruz bounded out of the bedroom. "My friend can't make it for half an hour. I think that might be too late." He threw a pad of paper and pen at me. "Write down everything you need, and where it's located in the apartment. I'll run over there now. You might have to stay here for a while."

I tilted my head and scowled. Was he for real? Hell no. I wasn't staying here.

"It's for your protection."

I gave him an eyeroll.

"Can't I go to my apartment myself to get what I need?"

Cruz shook his head. "It's too risky. If Luís' goons show up, I might be able to convince him that I was only there to try and hook up with you. They know how I am with the ladies, and we have a history."

This guy was so full of himself.

"They would believe you'd try to score with me and Rosa, the same night?"

He shrugged.

I shook my head. This guy was unbelievable. I knew I had been reckless. Another in the long list of mistakes I made since coming here. As arrogant as Cruz was, I could see his logic. Staying clear of Benjie's apartment would be the safe thing to do, especially if Luís knew where I lived. He had asked a lot of questions after he drugged me. I wasn't sure what I had told him. Not that I'd admit to Cruz he was right. The most important thing to me was Miles. I didn't want anything to happen to that sweet little kitten. Even though I wanted nothing more than to rip into Cruz for his bossy attitude and outrageous suggestions. Instead, I bit my tongue and focused on the list. My to-go bag had most of my essentials and some clothes. I wrote that along with mostly cat stuff, along with my laptop and jewelry kit. I may as well get some work done if I was stuck here. At least I didn't have to worry about Benjie's journal. That was hidden. I handed him the note.

He grabbed a rolling suitcase and whispered back and forth with Rosa for a few minutes. Why was I still being left in the dark? I started following him when he went for the front door.

"Stay out of sight, just in case. No one can know you're here. Understand?"

"I'm not stupid, you know. I just wanted to know how you'll get into my apartment. My purse is back in Luís' office, unless someone happened to grab it."

Rosa shook her head.

Cruz jingled his keyring.

I frowned.

"I have a copy of your apartment key."

"What?" My jaw dropped.

# ZIZI HART

This guy was unbelievable. The nerve of him. Making a copy of my key. When had he done that?

"Wait." I snatched back the note, and wrote one more item at the bottom. He glanced at the paper and paused. A smirk crossed his lips, and then he chuckled.

"Don't flatter yourself. It's not because of you." My face heated from embarrassment. I had written down birth control pills. They were in the medicine cabinet. Sue me for wanting some normalcy. Throwing off my cycle wouldn't do. In the scheme of things, it was a ridiculous request. But I didn't care. It was something I could control, and I desperately needed that right now.

He burst into laughter. I couldn't stand it. I stormed to the bathroom and slammed the door. The laughter rang in my ears long after he left. That bastard. Had he been searching my place since I got here? And what had he found rifling through all my personal stuff? What might he find there tonight? I wasn't ashamed of anything I had exactly, but I could do without him finding my stash of vibrators.

Rosa knocked on the door.

"I'm calling Dion's pizza. You got any preference for toppings?"

I opened the door and shook my head. My stomach was still queasy from whatever drug Luís had slipped in my drink. I went to the kitchen cupboard and found a glass. My hands were shaking as I filled it from the tap. I sat on the couch staring at the tv, watching the news but not fully absorbing anything. I felt numb. The couch cushions dipped beside me. Rosa was staring at me. I could feel it. She could have been asking me questions. I had no idea. I think I was in shock. I blinked back unshed tears and tried to focus. The buzzing noise in my head finally quieted.

"Mari honey, are you alright?"

Her voice was soft and soothing. It was similar to the voice I used to coax Miles into that box at the gas station. Suddenly I

## SANTA FE SEDUCTION

started to worry how Cruz would be able to get Miles out of the apartment. He liked to hide under my bed. I hadn't shared that information with him. I started searching for my phone, but realized it was still in my purse. The one that was still in Luís' office.

"Do you have Cruz' number?" I asked.

She unlocked her phone and tossed it to me. "Yeah, here you go."

I scrolled through her numbers and found Cruz. He picked up on the fourth ring breathing heavily, like he had just run a marathon.

"What?" He barked into the phone.

I stared at the phone pissed off he was giving me attitude. I had been through enough tonight. The nerve of this guy. I didn't need his shit on top of everything else.

"I called", I said through gritted teeth, "to let you now that Miles likes to hide under my bed inside my ASU sweatshirt."

"Sorry. Didn't mean to bite your head off. Let me put you on speaker phone. Maybe if he hears your voice, he'll come out."

It wasn't a bad idea. Maybe the egotistical pretty boy had a few braincells after all.

"Miles, sweetie. Here kitty. Come to mama. Come on out." I kept repeating soft words. "You're safe honey. Come on baby. It's ok." I heard a scuffle, then a grunt and swear words intermixed with high-pitched meow screeches blasting through the speaker.

"Don't hurt him." I whined.

It was clear from all the racket that the poor kitten was not happy with whatever was happening.

Cruz came back on the line breathing heavy. "Don't worry. He didn't hurt me."

"You do realize I was talking about Miles."

"Yeah, I know." I could hear the laughter in his voice. He was obviously poking fun and it grated on my nerves.

"Put Rosa on the line."

I handed the phone over to her and she took it off speaker. Still trying to hide things from me? Hadn't we moved past that? It was frustrating being out of the loop, but they had rescued me so I guess I should feel grateful. Or maybe they had only pretended to rescue me. Was that possible? My paranoia had me questioning everything. I didn't know who to trust, only that my judgement was severely lacking lately.

"He should be here in about 20 minutes with the pizza."

Time seemed to drag as we waited. I was worried about so many things, and had so many questions. Although, to be fair, I'm not sure I'd believe the answers at this point. I debated if I should even bother. It didn't take long before the internal nagging inside my brain won out.

"How did you know Luís was holding me in his office?"

Rosa shook her head slowly. What did that mean? Did she not want to think or talk about what happened? Could she not share the details? Would Cruz get mad if she did? They both knew more than they were sharing. I was hesitant to trust anyone at this point. I had trusted Luís and that had been a Huge Mistake. Rosa was related to Luís, which in my book meant they were close, and therefore conspiring together. That labeled her as an enemy. But I also knew that families could be complicated. My relationship with Benjie had been that way. I really wanted to give Rosa the benefit of the doubt, but… There was always a but.

Rosa's cell rang and we both jumped. She answered with a nervous giggle.

"Hey Cruz." She sighed. "Yeah. No problem. I'll make it look good."

Rosa bounded off the couch and started undressing. She laid her jeans on the back of the kitchen chair and unbuttoned her blouse. My eyes popped. What was going on? She bent over at the waist and shook her hair out, then flipped it back. The fly away curls looked super sexy. She looked like one of those models from

## SANTA FE SEDUCTION

those magazine's my step-father always kept hidden from my mom. Rosa left one lamp on by the door and turned off the rest.

"Stay clear of the doorway and don't make a sound."

Rosa flung open the door and stood in the entryway. Anyone looking at the apartment would be able to see her standing in the light. A half-naked sex goddess, waiting to be worshipped. She flung out a hip and struck a pose in her lace pushup bra and underwear. The unbuttoned blouse hid next to nothing. Her slim muscular legs were on full display.

"Well, hello, lover."

I peeked from the side of the couch at that comment. Lover? They were having sex.

"I got your bag and that pizza you wanted."

He stared at Rosa appreciatively and set the bag and pizza just inside the doorway.

The bag had barely touched the floor before she pounced. That's the only way I could describe what happened. I watched a lot of nature videos, and it was just like that. A cougar attacking its prey. I had to cover my mouth to keep from making a noise. They kissed and groped one another like they had done it a thousand times. I hadn't realized they were an item now. I guess I was wrong. About a lot of things. I felt a jolt of jealousy flow through my veins, and it pissed me off. I shouldn't care if he had a girlfriend or lover, or whatever they were to one another. I was confused which one of them to be more upset with. Cruz seemed to grate on my nerves regularly, but I had confided with Rosa on my plan to seduce Cruz. True it was only to use him to gather information, but Rosa hadn't known that part. Once again, I had gotten into trouble for trusting strangers. I needed to stop being so damn gullible.

They finally finished their grope fest for all to see, made their way into the apartment and closed the door. Rosa wiped her mouth and stared at me. Was she waiting for me to react? I wasn't going to give the two of them the satisfaction. She buttoned her blouse and slipped back into her jeans. I appreciated the modesty, regardless on it being too little, too late. Cruz looked like he wanted to say something but I shook my head. Whatever it was, I didn't want to hear it. I was barely holding it together. I only wanted one thing from him.

"Where is Miles?" I whispered.

The bag started moving. A little head peeked out from the zipper. That adorable little fluff ball seemed to reset everything. I had purpose once again. I would focus all my energy on Miles until I could figure out the rest. Again, that little guy was there to save me. Just like I had saved him. I unzipped the bag all the way and snuggled Miles to my chest. His soft vibrating purrs were a balm to my nerves. I ignored Rosa and Cruz as they set the table in the kitchen quietly whispering to one another. I grabbed the heavy suitcase and dragged it down the hallway to the spare bedroom.

"Don't use social media. It's dangerous." Cruz said. He tried to help with the bag, but I yanked it away from him. I lifted my head, put my nose in the air and turned.

"No thank you. I've got it." My voice sounded like broken shards of glass.

Broken. Kind of how my heart felt when witnessing Rosa and Cruz moments ago. I shook my head. Preposterous. Heart? Feelings? Up until now, it had only been a concoction of lust and hate. Cruz had jumbled my emotions from the very beginning. I was better than this. Stronger. I set Miles on the floor after closing the door. One day at a time. That was my mantra, and I wasn't about to let that change now.

# Chapter 13

*Cruz*

My cell phone rang waking me from a sound sleep. I glanced at the time. I must have drifted off. It was 10am. Rosa had left about an hour ago to head to the airport. I glanced at Mari still cuddled up on the couch. The kitten had crawled under the covers with her. His little face was peeking out at me

"Yeah." I answered. My voice sounded like I had gargled with gravel.

"Hey Cruz." Rosa said.

"Are you calling from the airport?"

"My flight was canceled."

I had checked her flight info myself. It was still on schedule. Had El Lobo Rojo found out we had been the ones to help Mari escape? My hand gripped the phone as my mind raced.

"Is Luís mad about last night?"

She huffed. "It's none of his business who I sleep with."

The fact that she said those words, told me she was putting on a show. More than likely, I was on speaker, and people were listening in.

"I don't want any trouble with the boss."

"It's fine."

# ZIZI HART

"So why are you calling?"

"Since I'm free, I was hoping we could go to breakfast."

"Yeah sure. When will you be ready? Do you want me to pick you up?"

"Nah. I can meet at your place. There's a fantastic pancake house around the corner. I can't remember the name, something like F&F on 11th."

I knew that was code. I just couldn't figure what it meant. F&F. Then I realized she always called Luís' bodyguards Frick and Frack. They must be on their way. Eleventh could have meant they were that many minutes away, or maybe they would be there at 11. I didn't have much time. The goons had started doing employee house searches earlier than I expected. I had to get Mari out of the apartment. Luckily, I had a neighbor who was out of town. I was cat sitting for her. I hoped Miles would get along with the woman's cat, because I didn't have an alternative.

"Not sure if that place is still in business. But I'll find us somewhere to go. I got it covered. See you soon."

I hung up the phone and rushed to Mari's side.

"Wake up." I gently shook her shoulder.

She blinked at me from the couch.

"Why? I just went to sleep a few hours ago."

"Luís' people will be here any minute. If they find you," I shivered. I didn't even want to think about what they would do. "They can't find you."

My tone was deadly. It got her moving. She went under the sink and grabbed a garbage bag. Anything she couldn't stuff in her backpack was thrown into the bag. It was all done within minutes. I had never seen anyone pack that quickly. It was as if she had done it before. No one could be that fast without practice. What had her life been like before this? If we survived the day, I promised myself to ask her. Mari was waiting for me at the front door with Miles.

# SANTA FE SEDUCTION

"My neighbor is out of town. You can stay there until I know it's clear."

She nodded. "Show me the way."

It was on the same level, just across from my apartment. I glanced to see if the goons had arrived yet. No one suspicious was in the parking lot. I crossed to my neighbor's apartment and unlocked the door. I held it open and she was inside within seconds. I didn't waste time making sure she was comfortable. I had to double-check everything was in order at my place.

Luís' goons José and Bruno arrived at 11. That had given me extra time to stash any evidence of work from my real job. The apartment was clean. They wouldn't find anything out of the ordinary.

José and Bruno stood at my door looking sheepish.

"Hey Cruz." José said.

I looked between the two of them.

"What's up?"

"Boss said we had to do a search of everyone's home."

"Why?" I asked.

They looked at one another. "It's orders."

"Fine. Whatever." I tossed Bruno my apartment key. "Lock up when you're done and slip the key under the mat. I'm taking Rosa to breakfast."

I knew they would report everything they found along with my cavalier attitude toward the whole business back to El Lobo Rojo. It should prove I had nothing to hide.

Rosa pulled into the parking lot and honked. I waved.

"Don't make too much of a mess guys. I might be bringing Rosa back upstairs for another round." I wiggled my eyebrows.

They gave deep masculine chuckles.

I hoped that put their minds at ease, that I couldn't be connected to Mari's disappearance. The only trouble was, once they had searched everyone's residence, and found nothing, what would they do? I needed a scape goat, but I couldn't in good

85

conscious offer up anyone knowing that person would be tortured and killed. We needed to come up with some plausible way that Mari could have escaped on her own, or had some outside help, one that couldn't be pinpointed. I wasn't about to add someone else to the long list of people El Lobo Rojo had killed. He had a reputation. No one crossed him and lived to talk about it.

 The drive to the restaurant was subdued. We weren't sure if her car had been bugged. We were both afraid to talk just in case someone was listening. Any conversation was stilted, and filled with code. We both left our phones in the car. Neither one of us thought we had been followed, but I searched the restaurant and gave her the signal when it was ok to talk. We found a corner booth.

 The waitress came over to take our order.

 "What'll you have?"

 "Two Coffees, black. I'll have a skillet." I gestured to Rosa.

 "I'll have the giant cinnamon roll."

 My eyebrows rose. She usually watched her weight. Those cocktail waitress outfits were ridiculously skimpy.

 "Don't give me that look pendejo. I need sugar when I'm stressed."

 I held up my hands in surrender. "I'm not saying a word. I think we should be ok to talk here."

 She sighed. "Luís is losing his mind searching for her."

 "I figured as much."

 "Where did you stash her?" She shook her head. "Wait. I don't want to know."

 "Has he gone through the video footage yet?"

 "He's having his guys go through it now. But he's not going to find anything."

 "Why not?"

 "Luís took out the surveillance cameras in his office and the ones at the back of the building are just for show. That's where he does his dirty work. He doesn't trust anyone with access to recordings that might implicate him."

I was grateful for the lucky break. If Luís had witnessed Rosa and I leaving with the giant suitcase he might have been more suspicious. Now that I knew of the secret sliding door, that might give me an opportunity to plant a camera in his office. I had gathered plenty of audio over the last six months, but I hadn't been able to do the same with video. Luís was always careful how he presented himself in public.

The waitress dropped off the coffees. We waited until she was gone before picking up our conversation.

"What happened with your trip to Columbia? I know the flight wasn't canceled."

"It's my own fault. I left my passport at the club in my locker. It was stupid, but I hadn't been thinking clearly last night."

"What happened when you got to the club this morning?"

"Luís yanked me into his office for an interrogation. He decided it was too much of a coincidence that I was heading on a trip out of the country, right after the girl went missing." She snickered. "He was probably more pissed that I got to go home, while he was stuck here. Luís always was a selfish jerk."

"He can't go back to Columbia?"

Did Luís have some sort of travel restriction? If so, that was news to me.

"No. He can't."

"Is he on the no-fly list?"

She chuckled. "The U.S. doesn't restrict his movements." Rosa bit her lip, and looked around. No one was listening. "I'm going to share something with you, but you have to swear not to tell a soul."

"Of course."

"It has nothing to do with the government. The Mendoza family is the reason Luís can't go back to Columbia."

I sat back in the booth. Another notorious drug family was after Luís?

"What happened?"

"Luís worked with Felipe Mendoza. No one knows all the details, but they were doing a job and everything went sideways. Felipe ended up shot. Most believe that Luís pulled the trigger. Everyone knows Luís' is psychotic, and that the two of them had been arguing, but nothing could be proven. The gun was never found." She shrugged. "A deal was struck between the two older Lorenzo brothers and Mario Mendoza. Luís would leave the country and could start up business in the states, but it couldn't be in any territory owned by the Mendoza family. Since Mario controls Albuquerque, Luís chose Santa Fe as his home base."

I had always wondered why El Lobo Rojo had chosen Santa Fe. Now I knew. It hadn't been random.

"It's close enough to Albuquerque."

"But far enough away to maintain the parameters of the agreement."

"The two families work together amicably?"

She snorted. "Loose alliance at best. But they try not to kill one another. Luckily, Felipe was not a favorite cousin of Mario's, or he wouldn't have been so forgiving."

Luís pissed off people on a regular basis. He was dangerous. We needed to get him put away before he started a turf war. I couldn't imagine the number of civilian casualties if that happened.

The waitress dropped off our food, and scurried away. I dug into my skillet like it was my last meal. Rosa took delicate bites with her fork.

"So, what did you talk about when you were in Luís' office?"

"He wanted a blow by blow of yesterday's events. I told him mostly the truth. After work, I went home with you and stayed at your place until morning. He knew you've been hitting on me

## SANTA FE SEDUCTION

ever since you started at the club, so it didn't seem strange for me to finally give in and sleep with you."

"What were you going back to Columbia for?"

"I was going to visit Luís' sister, well actually her grave. She died a few years back. And then I was going to visit a few friends. The trip was just for the weekend, but he told me it was canceled. He couldn't allow me to leave." She let out a long breath. "He made up some bullshit excuse that a few waitresses had called in sick and he needed me to be there." She snorted. "That's such bullshit."

"He didn't question the huge bag? Surely Bruno and José would have said something. That was a large bag for such a short trip."

"Oh please. I always pack like I'm going to be gone for months. I don't want to forget anything." She shrugged. "It's not a real suitcase if you can't fit a dead body. I think that was one of my grandfather's sayings."

"Quite the colorful family motto."

"I've got dozens of quotes, and the stories I could tell, you wouldn't believe. I could fill a book."

I just bet she could. The Lorenzos were infamous. We both agreed to keep our cool and go about business as usual until the heat died down.

# Chapter 14

### Mari

Only three days had passed while hiding out in Cruz's apartment, but it felt like weeks. I was going completely stir crazy. He refused to tell me anything about his job at Club Cuervo or what he had planned to get us all out of this mess. Of course that didn't stop him from asking me questions, like what my relationship was to BJ. I guess I had never told him he was my brother. I don't know what he had assumed, but my answer seemed to satisfy him.

I'd gotten sick of our one-sided conversations. The only question he was willing to answer was what was going on between himself and Rosa. He had told me it was nothing. That first night had been an act for those watching the apartment. Not that I believed him one hundred percent, because I had witnessed him flirt with her, as well as countless others at the club. I was ashamed to admit that it pleased me to know he couldn't take a new girl home from the club every night. That's how Rosa described his normal 'dating routine'.

Since I was living in his apartment, I was delighted to be cramping his style. It opened up the opportunity to pursue my original plan of seduction. Not that I had been successful. Cruz still hadn't parted with any useful information, but I was going to double down my efforts tonight. The sexual tension between us was strung so tight, it felt like a stiff breeze could break it. Of course I wasn't allowed to feel a breeze these days. I couldn't open the windows or put a pinky toe out of the apartment. Standing too close to the blinds would cause Cruz to have an aneurism.

I heard the key turn in the deadbolt and froze in place, hiding in the hallway. I peeked around the corner and breathed a sigh of relief when I saw who it was. He was back from the club early. Cruz thew his over-shirt on the chair and collapsed onto the couch. He remained that way for several minutes without moving a muscle, with his head back and eyes closed.

I was an absolute bundle of nerves. I had been thinking of what to do all night. I couldn't wait another second. I stepped into the living room trying to play it cool.

I leaned against the wall trying to look sexy in nothing but a silk dress shirt I had found in his closet.

His eyes popped open, and they darkened and sparkled with interest. Cruz leaned forward.

I sauntered over to the coffee table moving the shirt like a breeze was blowing indoors. First the right, then the left side. Flashing and covering my essentials as I approached.

"So, still nothing going on between you and Rosa?" I needed to hear it one more time, to reassure myself.

He shook his head.

"Prove it." I flipped back both sides of the shirt, and settled down on the coffee table, crossing my legs. There was a hair breadth between us, and I was dying to close that gap. I had his full attention, despite the obvious exhaustion from moments before.

"How exactly do I do that?" His voice had deepened.

I leaned back on my elbows, uncrossing my legs, giving him full access to see or do what he wanted with me.

"Use your imagination." I quirked a brow.

# SANTA FE SEDUCTION

Cruz wiped his hand over his mouth as he stared at me.

I was sprawled on the coffee table virtually naked, shaking with anticipation. I had never done anything so bold in my entire life.

His eyes were tactile as they roamed my body. It felt like minutes as I sat there, but was probably only moments. Time had slowed to a crawl. Say something to me already, I screamed in my head. Touch me. Anything.

Cruz stood and walked to kitchen. I felt crushed to my core. I couldn't believe it. I had been coming on to him for the better part of a week, and every time he walked away a little more of my self-esteem flushed down the toilet. What was I doing wrong? I knew my body wasn't perfect, but I thought I looked pretty good. No guy had ever turned me down, especially with the level of effort I was putting in. I knew I couldn't have imagined the chemistry between us. He had said he wasn't involved with Rosa. I just couldn't figure out what the problem was. In the past, all I had to do was look at a guy. Hell, usually all I had to do was breathe in a guy's direction, and he was all over me. But for some reason Cruz was different, which didn't make any sense at all, since the guy hit on everything in a skirt. I was starting to develop a complex. I never had insecurities before, but with him, they were coming out full force. That bastard. I needed to change tactics. Get him to react.

"Are you gay?"

"What?"

"Well, you must have just come out of the closet, if you're no longer interested."

Cruz's expression was priceless. "I have hit on almost every woman at the club. Have you ever seen me hitting on the guys?"

"No, but maybe you were converted recently?"

He shook his head. "Why are you doing this?"

I closed the shirt and grabbed the blanket off the back of the couch covering myself like it could somehow shield my broken ego. I felt like such a fool. I stole his spot and sunk into the cushions hoping the couch would engulf me. At least it was more comfortable than the coffee table.

He stood there with his hands on his hips. Wasn't it obvious why I was doing this? Did I really have to spell it out for him?

"Why do you think, Cruz? You're the one with all the answers, and I'm left with nothing."

## Chapter 15

*Cruz*

I stormed to my bedroom and slammed the door. Mari was impossible. Didn't she realize how hard I was fighting the attraction between us? She had been kidnapped. Or almost. I cringed thinking what might have happened. Didn't she realize the danger she was in? The anger boiled in my blood, and I drove a fist into the wall. She was nothing but a distraction. I was already too involved with her, and we hadn't even slept together. Luís had become insanely paranoid, emphasis on the insane, and was taking his frustrations out on everyone at the club. His overly suspicious attitude was making my job nearly impossible. He was still looking for the accomplice, the traitor that helped Mari escape. Luís assumed correctly that it had been someone on the inside. By the time I finished the rant in my head, I stared at the sizable hole I had left in the drywall. My hand was killing me. In the bathroom I ran cool water over my scraped knuckles.

Not sharing information with her was a way to distance myself at least partly. I had to keep things professional. Or as much as I could. I was keeping her in the dark for a reason. If she knew exactly what El Lobo Rojo would have done to her, it would cause her to panic, or crumble. I desperately wanted to hit another wall, but what would that accomplish? More pain, and more damage. I should have gotten out some of my frustration at the gym, but I wanted to get back to the apartment as soon as possible after work, to make sure she was safe.

I was obviously glutton for punishment, since being around Mari was a constant tease. Her quest for answers, and the way she was going about it. I would have welcomed those come-ons in any other scenario. I was worried that Mari would become so frustrated that she might try to seek answers on her own and leave the safety of the apartment. It's not like I had her locked up. She was free to go if she wanted.

That's another reason why I hadn't filled her in on my plans. She could jeopardize everything if she left and was captured. I couldn't bear that happening. Mari tended to be hot-headed. It was one of the things that had attracted me. All that passion bottled up in that petite little package. I sighed. Maybe I should throw her a bone and give her something. Anything, so she would ease up on the interrogations. I didn't need her doing something stupid, like sneaking out.

I exited the bedroom and walked to the kitchen. Mari had gotten dressed. She was working on her laptop. I wondered if I should remind her to not use social media. The look she flashed me told me to keep my trap shut. I went to the fridge and poured some iced tea.

"Do you want some?"

Mari blinked. "Yeah. On your head."

My lips twitched, and I forced myself not to grin. That would only encourage her. God love her, but she was entertaining.

I took a long drink. "Maybe it's you who needs to cool off?"

"Don't even go there. I heard you punch the wall back there. You think your bedroom is sacred when you leave? Between the two of us, it's you that needs a cold shower."

# SANTA FE SEDUCTION

I didn't realize she was exploring my bedroom when I left, but I should have. Mari was more curious than most. Now that's all I would be thinking about. Her rolling in my sheets. No wonder I smelled her scent on my pillow. She was correct about an icy shower. My body was strung so tight from the tension of the job, the worry about Mari, and with the sexual electricity between us, I knew something had to give, and soon.

"I think I'll take a shower."

I waited for her to make some suggestive remark. She had been doing that every chance she got. I imagined stripping her out of that oversized t-shirt. Peeling off those skinny jeans and taking my sweet time washing every inch of her body. Would she be willing to reciprocate? The thought of her soft fingers roaming all over me was getting me harder by the second. Her eyes met mine. She sighed and turned away, focusing on her laptop. I didn't want to admit how many times this past week, I had almost given into temptation. I was trying to be noble, and professional, trying to be César Ramirez, the man she didn't know, and it was killing me. I kept hoping she would grow bored or frustrated, and she would give up this relentless pursuit. It appeared I might have gotten my wish, but it filled me with nothing but regret. What if I asked her to join me? It was something my alias, Cruz Diaz would have done in a heartbeat. What could it hurt? It didn't mean I had to tell her about my job. We could scratch that itch, we both desperately needed. I know I was coming up with excuses, trying to convince myself, regardless how unethical it was.

I started toward the bathroom, but made a turn back to the kitchen to rest the now empty glass in the sink. Mari wasn't typing. Her eyes had glazed over like she wasn't reading what was on the screen. She was pretending, but I knew better. Her breathing sped up as I rounded the table, coming up behind her. Fuck protocol.

"The shower is big enough for two."

She sucked in a breath.

I strolled to the bathroom. Invitation sent. The next move was hers.

# Chapter 16

*Mari*

He wanted me. The message crystal clear. I must have worn him down. I had been working to get to this point for the past week. Why was I hesitating? Had I lost my nerve? I licked my suddenly dry lips. This was after all, to get all the information I needed. I pondered on everything I wanted to know. My mind was a complete blank. Oh, who was I kidding, I was about to see this guy naked. A giggle of excitement escaped before I could help it. I looked around hoping he hadn't heard that ridiculous sound. Thankfully he had already closed the door.

    I gathered my courage, pushed back my shoulders and approached the bathroom and listened. He hadn't turned on the water yet. Was he waiting for me? I bit my bottom lip and turned the knob. Cruz was facing the mirror standing with his back to me. He was completely undressed. His clothes were probably in a pile somewhere, but my whole world narrowed down to the perfection in front of me. Caramel skin with zero body fat. Broad shoulders. Lean, toned muscles. He had a lot more tattoos covering his body that I hadn't seen with his clothes on, but nothing was graphic or distasteful. Most were tribal tattoos, that adorned and accented every muscle on his body. And this was just his backside.

He stared at me through the mirror. His smile was smug. He must have known I wouldn't pass up this opportunity. He was such an ass. I lowered my gaze. Speaking of, the cocky SOB had a perfectly round tight ass, that led to equally chiseled thighs. It figured. This guy could definitely be a model. I'd buy anything he was selling. At this point, I wasn't sure I could take the view from the front. I might pass out. In fact, I was feeling a little lightheaded. He turned and I had to lean against the wall. The tattoos continued around to the front, and woah mama. I wanted to lick every inch of him. I wondered what he would say if I stated exactly what I was thinking.

"Are you dirty?" He asked.

My thoughts certainly were.

"Did you come for that shower, or do you want to hop in with your clothes on?"

I suddenly felt shy. My body couldn't compare to his. I didn't work out much. Well, to be honest, I barely went to the gym. I was slender, but not really toned. My hesitation didn't make logical sense. The guy had already seen me naked. I had flaunted myself this past week. Plus, there was that night he took me home. I still didn't know if we had slept together.

"Here. I'll help you."

He reached for my sweatshirt, and I was too dumbfounded to do anything. It's like I had lost the ability to speak. His beauty made me mute.

He slid the bulky thing off. Of course, he didn't realize that one of the bags he had grabbed from my closet last week had some seriously sexy undergarments stashed in the hidden pockets. I had taken to wearing them under my day clothes, in hopes for just such an occasion.

His expression of shock at my black lace push-up bra made me grin.

He wiped a hand down his face. "I didn't expect. Uh. Wow."

I needed that boost of confidence. It gave me the equalizer I needed to finish what I started.

I turned and gave him a view of my backside and shimmied out of my jeans.

His breath went out of him like a hiss as he stared at the matching black lace thong.

I knew my ass looked fantastic, or at least that's what past boyfriends had told me.

I glanced over my shoulder at Cruz. His eyes were glued to that particular asset. I gave one cheek a slap and his eyes met mine.

They twinkled and filled with mischief.

He grabbed me and threw me into the shower, and I yelped. But then his lips were on mine, and I couldn't do anything but feel his hard body pressing into mine. I still had my bra and panties on, but I didn't care. He was touching me. Finally. It was as if a dam had been released. Cruz took his sweet time, and it was driving me crazy. I wanted him to hurry and get to the good stuff. I was ready to rip into him, and then his lips suckled my nipple, and I felt myself coming undone. He slid his fingers into my panties, and I rubbed against him like I was a cat in heat. I couldn't believe how turned on I was. I had never felt so totally out of control.

"Please." I moaned. I didn't even know what I was asking for, but he seemed to understand.

"Anything Mari." He kissed my lips, my neck. "Everything." He whispered.

I was shaking, so desperate to come.

Cruz knelt in the tub and grabbed the edge of the thong and pulled it to the side. He licked the cream, and my head fell back against the tile. I know I was making some animalistic sound, but I didn't have any dignity left. He had stolen it from me.

## ZIZI HART

I was his for the taking. He took his time. Coaxing me. Teasing me. When he finally let me come, I had my legs wrapped around his shoulders, and my upper back balanced against the wall of the shower. I should have been concerned about crashing to the porcelain, but all I could do was blink back the tears in my eyes and sigh. My body felt liquid, like I could collapse into a puddle of goo at any moment. I was utterly boneless. Cruz chuckled. I leaned against him as he stripped me of my panties and bra, too weak to even help. He turned on the shower. He soaped up the washcloth and rubbed me all over, spending extra time on certain overly sensitive areas. Each rub of the cloth brought after-shocks of pleasure to the point of almost pain.

"I can't take it." I squirmed, trying to get away from his touch.

"You will," His voice deepened as he gripped my hips. "We're just getting started."

I didn't know how to respond. He was so bossy, and sexy. Normally I wouldn't tolerate that kind of attitude, but as I stared into his eyes, I realized I trusted him, even though I had no reason to.

"You must have really needed that."

"You have no idea," I said.

It had been almost a year since I had been with someone, and as stimulating as my vibrators were, there was no substitute for a lover, especially one who was so skilled. I thought briefly on how he had acquired those skills, but I couldn't muster up any emotion except gratitude. When he finished washing me, I was able to fully stand on my own, and was anxious to reciprocate.

I bit my lip as he stood in front of me. I didn't think he could look any more magnificent. Water streamed down his tatted muscles. My voice caught in my throat. I couldn't form words. I knelt in the tub, not caring that it made my hair plaster to my scalp. I took him into my mouth.

# SANTA FE SEDUCTION

"Mari." He breathed.

I could tell he wanted to grab my head, but Cruz was trying to be gentle. I watched the strain in his body and the tight fist he wrapped in the shower curtain. It allowed me to push past my comfort zone, and give him what he needed. Fast and hard. He had pleasured me, and I wanted to do the same. I was more than willing. I curled my hands around him as I sucked and watched with satisfaction when his eyes rolled back. His release seemed to go on and on. The expression he gave me after was priceless. It held such surprise and wonder. The intense way he stared at me, like he had never really seen me before now. That look. I could easily become addicted.

# Chapter 17

*Cruz*

After drying each other off, I took Mari back to the bedroom. I'm sure the neighbors would complain about the noise in the morning, but I didn't care. I wasn't going to be there much longer. She was such a revelation. It took my breath away. There was something about her bold passion mixed with vulnerability that managed to hit all my buttons. Mari snuggled closer to my side until she was practically purring with satisfaction. Or maybe that was Miles. He was in the bedroom somewhere watching. That kitten was cute, but then again, so was Mari. They were both small, with spunky attitudes. They were perfect for one another. I didn't know exactly where I fit into the mix, but it felt right with her in my arms. I knew better than get involved, but I couldn't seem to resist. We hadn't even had sex yet. I sighed, giving her a tight squeeze and tried to roll away. Mari hugged tighter, like I was a favorite stuffed toy she wasn't quite ready to part with.

"Mari, honey. I need to get up."

She made some incoherent reply that had me grinning. As much as I didn't want to move, I needed to finish up my plans, or there would be no tomorrow, for either of us. We were running out of time. El Lobo Rojo was on edge. More people had been coming into his office for meetings. His security had tightened. I knew something was going down soon, but he had been close-lipped about his plans with almost everyone, ever since Mari's escape. I hadn't been able to get into his office to tap his phone and put in a camera. As soon as an opportunity presented itself, I would do that. I was desperate to wrap up this assignment. Maybe then, I could really explore whatever this thing was between Mari and myself. That is, if she could still trust me. I gave another half-hearted attempt to separate our bodies. She resisted. I knew Mari was awake, otherwise I would have easily broken free. She must really need to be held to keep up the charade. I wrapped my arms around her, snuggling in. The sigh she released made it worth it. In the past, I would have never allowed a woman to get this close. Sex was fine, and maybe some cuddling after, but never sleep. That was too risky. I'd be far too helpless. I needed to stay vigilant for danger. That was my job. I gave a huge yawn. Maybe I could make an exception, allow myself a reprieve. Just this once. I don't know how Mari managed to do the impossible, but I felt myself drifting off to sleep in her arms. When I woke three hours later, I was shocked. I never fell this soundly asleep. I had insomnia most nights. I would wake in cold sweats to nightmares, but instead I felt warm and relaxed, and content. When had I ever felt content? I tried to unpeel our limbs from one another.

"Don't leave." She whispered.

"I didn't realize you were awake." I gave Mari a quick kiss to the forehead. "I have to."

I needed to somehow take charge of this situation, before it got any further out of control.

She tightened her grip around my waist like that could somehow stop me, but then her body started moving, and I lost all train of thought. I rolled her over and continued to slide over her until we were both panting.

"I need you inside." She whispered.

## SANTA FE SEDUCTION

I reached my hand down and felt for her opening. Mari was dripping wet. I didn't need any further proof that she had been awake for a while now and thinking about this. Us.

"Condom." I croaked and rolled to the bedside table. I slipped it on, and positioned myself on shaky arms at her entrance. Her thighs clenched and she made this sound halfway between a sigh and a groan as I entered her. That sound flipped a switch deep within me. I wanted to hear it over and over. That excited half breath, that told me I was everything to her in that moment. That sound was pure adrenaline. She ran her hands over my pecs, around my shoulders to my back, encouraging me to move. I had been waiting for that signal. I didn't want to hurt her, despite how wet she was. Mari was small, and I was definitely not.

"Cruz, I'm gonna need you to move." She bounced her hips.

I gritted my teeth. "Fuck Mari."

"Yes. Exactly Cruz. Fuck. Me."

I pounded into her. And she lost the ability for speech. I can't believe she was teasing me. Testing me. I was going to show her. She was making more of those sounds, and I was making my own. I was savage. Pure animal. She brought out the worst, or in her words best in me. I was brutal taking her, but she met me thrust for thrust. It wasn't too much for her despite my size. Mari had claws. Her cute little sharp nails that she dug into my backside. It spurred me on. She lost her rhythm and I knew she was close. Her eyes rolled back in her head, and her breath caught.

"Come for me, Mari." I changed up the tempo, lengthening my thrusts. It was sending her over the edge, and I wanted to join her. I had zero self-preservation where she was concerned.

Pounding her into the bed, we found our release together.

I stayed connected, not wanting to leave her warmth for a few moments, our hearts pounding in unison.

# ZIZI HART

"That's the way I want to wake up, for the rest of my life." Mari hugged me tighter. I hadn't thought we could get any closer, but she managed to make our bodies meld together. I felt a bond with this woman. It was something I didn't want to think about too clearly, but my brain wasn't listening. That statement had me contemplating the possibilities. I had never even considered being with a woman longer than a night or two. Even in high school, I hadn't gone steady. I was always distracted by the next pretty thing to walk by. Plus, my work didn't really allow for long-term commitments.

"Say something Cruz." She shook me. "Or have I fucked you speechless."

I chuckled.

"Oooh, stop that." She complained.

I was still inside her, shaking her body with my laughter.

"I'm tender. You dick."

I pulled out and rolled her to my side. One of her legs rested on my hip.

"I'm sorry. I can't help it. You're a regular comedian."

"It's my job to amuse." She smirked.

My smile faded as I started thinking how little I had laughed these past six months. Humor had been the furthest thing from my mind. El Lobo Rojo was on a rampage looking for the one that escaped. Finding out who the traitor was. Here I was enjoying myself, and danger surrounded us, ready to engulf us at any moment. I wasn't giving any of this, the attention it deserved. I had seen life snuffed out during my job. Life was so precious, and so easily taken. I curved my rough hand over her cheek. She was so soft. My thumb brushed against her lip. I couldn't bare for something to happen to her. I had caved to my own weakness, not thinking about the big picture. People were counting on me and I couldn't let them down.

# SANTA FE SEDUCTION

"What's with the sourpuss expression?" Mari asked. She had been staring at me, while I was lost in my thoughts. "You're killing my high."

I quirked a brow. Was she a drug user, like her brother?

"My orgasm high." She shoved at my shoulder.

How did she know what I was thinking? I had trained myself to keep a neutral expression. Once again, she undermined all my careful preparation with ease. Mari was dangerous. I went to get up, and she gripped my arm.

"Stay in bed." She pleaded with her eyes. "Please."

"I need to do some work on the computer."

"Do you ever sleep?"

"Maybe a couple of hours a night." I shrugged. "My work keeps me busy."

"That second job you won't talk about?"

My lips pressed together. I know that had been her plan. To seduce me, so I would talk. But it was still dangerous for her to know anything. What if she decided to leave? It wasn't like I was keeping her tied up. As much fun as that would be to have her in my bed, at my disposal, waiting for me to pleasure her, neither of us could afford that kind of freedom right now. I needed to focus. If she slipped up somehow, or freaked out and left the apartment and God forbid, was captured, it would be my life as well as hers. Because I would do anything to get her back. Not that I could tell her any of that. She didn't need to be frightened, or rather more frightened than she already was. Let her think whatever she wanted. Her imagination couldn't be worse than the truth. It was safer, for everyone.

She rolled over with a sigh.

I missed the softness of her curves and the warmth of her body immediately. I pulled her back against me. She struggled, but it was a pitiful effort. Mari needed my touch. I wouldn't deny her. I convinced myself I was only doing this for her. It had nothing to do with my own selfish wishes to hug her close to my

chest, allowing this illusion to wash over us, keeping this bubble of protection for just a little longer.
"Fine. I'll stay. Another hour. How's that?"
"Don't do me any favors."
I smacked her butt.
"Oww." She squirmed against me. "What was that for?"
"For being sassy." I rubbed the sting of the spank, massaging her ass, rolling onto my back, so she was sprawled on top of me.
"You're so bossy." She swatted my chest.
My lips curled. "Go to sleep."
She grumbled, but snuggled on top of me. In moments, she was softly snoring. I rubbed her back, making delicate circles, wondering what kind of future we had. Was that even possible with my line of work?

# Chapter 18

*Cruz*

I jumped as I heard an explosion of glass shattering into thousands of pieces. It pierced the quiet of the club as workers prepped in silence for the evening.

Luís had been smashing things in his office and swearing in Spanish for some time now. It was still hours before we opened, so no one but his most loyal employees would overhear his temper tantrum. Everyone knew to stay clear, when he was in one of his moods. But this level of anger was off the charts. The tension was so thick, the air was stifling.

"Joder!"

Another glass shattering.

"Puta Madre!"

The thud of something heavy being knocked over.

I sighed. Ramón would probably be asked to clean up the mess in Luís' office when his tirade ended, which meant I couldn't count on his help for prep work for much longer. Luckily, we had time. Ramón and I gathered supplies in the storage closet as quietly as we could. We knew any noise might set Luís off. I didn't want to be this close to the insanity normally. He was bound to do something unpredictable and deadly. The only spark of hope

## ZIZI HART

I had was that today I'd catch it all on video. I had managed to sneak into his office earlier to plant a small camera on a frame. It was sending wireless video to the laptop in my car. The thin secret door in the closet, meant we had an audio advantage to the conversation that those in the main bar did not. Ramón was visibly shaking.

"You incompetent gilipollas!" Luís yelled.

"What's with the plastic? Are you remodeling?" One of the new goons asked.

"Shut the fuck up." Another goon said.

"You can't find one single chocho!"

"Sorry Lobo Rojo. We've searched everywhere."

"Vete a la mierda!" Luís yelled.

A gunshot blast, and a loud thud hitting plastic.

Ramón and I glanced at one another holding our breaths. I wasn't sure if he knew about the sliding panel or not, but I knew for certain, I didn't want to be anywhere near it when they had to move the body. That kind of knowledge was dangerous. As it was, we had heard way too much. I just hoped the hidden camera in his office had recorded the whole thing. I wouldn't be able to check out the feed until later.

We were back in the bar stacking glasses and polishing the bar when Luís came out of his office.

"Ramón!" He yelled.

"Sí, Lobo Rojo."

Ramón sprinted to his uncle.

I overheard Luís asking him to sweep up some glass. I couldn't see the hallway that led to his office from my vantage, but that was just fine by me. The rest of the men from Columbia all stood a little taller. Alert. Respectful. That was the best way to describe them. I don't know if Luís had killed the guy because of his incompetence or to make a point to the rest. He didn't tolerate failure. El Lobo Rojo led by fear. Rosa glanced at me. There were no snide remarks or witty quips, which was unusual for her. From

# SANTA FE SEDUCTION

the stiffness in her shoulders as she moved about the club, I could tell she felt the pressure building around us. El Lobo Rojo was showing his true colors. His facade was cracking. Before long, the club would be splattered with red. I couldn't finish my assignment soon enough. I had worked other jobs like this and knew when it was time to run. It was long past that point, but I refused to give up when I was so close.

Lights flashed. The bass from the music thumped. Bodies rubbed against one another in a sea of cologne infused suffocation. In my youth this is where I had always wanted to be. Amongst the throng of people having fun, enjoying every moment. I gave a self-deprecating chuckle. I was in my early thirties, but my thoughts, they were ones of an old man. I had grown weary of this business. A police psychologist had warned me this might happen. It was a natural progression. The nature of my job. I had blown her off. That sort of thing would never happen to me. I was too controlled. Too in my head to let anything like depression bring me down. Boy, was I wrong.

In the VIP section, influential men surrounded Luís. He stood in a freshly pressed gray pinstriped suit. It was some high-end designer I couldn't pronounce let alone afford. His salt n' pepper hair was slicked back. From the outside Luís Lorenzo looked like an upstanding businessman, and impeccable dresser. He was suave and sophisticated. He joked with politicians, said all the right things to all the important people. He was charming. Even his Columbian accent was muted to fit in with the crowd. The human population. A group he had no right to be a part of. There was no doubt in my mind what he really was. An animal. His nickname fit. El Lobo Rojo. The red wolf. He left a pile of bodies in his path, as his empire grew. I wondered if the mayor knew what he was capable of. Did the judges and politicians he had befriended have a clue how easily he could kill? Like he had just killed the guy in cold blood a few hours ago in his office. José and Bruno were missing. That could only mean one thing. They

# ZIZI HART

were burying the body. Getting rid of any evidence. Luís didn't trust anyone else to take care of loose ends.

Ramón dropped off containers of olives and cherries, refilling the empty trays.

"You want to mix some drinks tonight?" I asked him.

He shook his head, eyes averted. I wondered if Ramón had seen the dead body earlier. Or had they already cleared it from the office? What had Luís said to the boy as he swept up the glass? Had Ramón been asked to clean up the blood? Or had the plastic tarp caught it all? No telling what the boy had witnessed. Ramón didn't seem to be in the mood to talk. At least the kid was lucky. He was family and Luís liked him. Ramón was his favorite nephew. He had mentioned that on numerous occasions. It may have been because he was such a hard-worker, and respectful. The kid looked up to his uncle. That's why he had sent for him when BJ died. Ramón was Maria's only son, El Lobo Rojo's sister. I had once asked about the family dynamic. It had been a mistake. An innocent question about his mother. Ramón had crossed himself. He told me his mother had passed a few years ago. He hadn't wanted to talk about the circumstances. Rosa had given the kid a hug, but then Ramón had rushed into the back for supplies. It had been a clear attempt not to cry in front of us. Being the brave solider. I had seen the tears welling in his eyes. He was a sensitive kid. I felt bad for him. He had been born into a ruthless family. The Lorenzo's were notorious. Colombian Mafiosos known for their brutality. Rosa stared at the kid as he gathered up dirty glasses in silence and walked toward the kitchen. She shared a look with me, pain in her eyes. We both wanted to help Ramón. He was an innocent, despite the Lorenzo name. But I couldn't think of a way out for him without blowing my cover.

# SANTA FE SEDUCTION

After work I stopped at the same fast-food place where Mari and I had met. I wasn't sure if she would be up or not, but I got us both burritos just in case. I called Jac while waiting in line and he answered on the third ring.

"What happened?" He cleared his throat.

"Did I wake you from your beauty sleep?"

"Fuck you. It's 3am."

"Love ya too, man." I needed something light-hearted to laugh about and banter with my best friend was about as good as it got.

"Don't keep me in suspense."

I guess I was hesitating on what I had to share.

"Someone died."

Silence filled the line.

"It wasn't anyone important. Just some thug from Columbia."

"That's scary you put it like that." Jac said, "You've been doing undercover for too long."

He was probably right. This job was burning me out. The excitement had lost its appeal long ago. All that remained was a whole lot of stress and danger. I often disassociated myself from the events around me. It was necessary to survive undercover as long as I did. If you showed emotions, they could be used as leverage, or worse get you killed. I filled Jac in on the facts from the case and shoved the rest of my thoughts down deep to analyze much later. I just needed to complete the assignment and get the evidence we needed, before my luck was shot to hell.

# Chapter 19

*Mari*

Cruz was gone again for work. He seemed to be leaving the apartment earlier and earlier every day. He wasn't around long enough to talk about anything. It pissed me off something fierce. Oh, he had time to wake me up in the middle of the night to make love to me, soft and sweet, or rough and hard. Whatever he needed. Don't get me wrong, I was always willing. And because my body was a fucking traitor, I let him make it sing every night without question. Then he would hold me until the morning like he'd never let me go. It felt like he cared. But he was hiding something. Something big. His eyes betrayed his words, or what few he shared with me. I was supposed to be getting all the details about Benjie, and the club's operations, or that had been my plan from the beginning. I needed to wrap my head around my brother's death. Didn't Cruz understand how necessary that was for my sanity? I knew he wanted to protect me from Luís, from whatever was going on at Club Cuervo. He and Rosa had rescued me from a dangerous situation. I got that. But leaving me in the dark was affecting my mental health. After years of therapy dealing with the trauma of an abusive step-father, I knew that physical protection would only get you so far. The mental aspect was the bigger hurdle. But anytime I would start to ask questions, he would suddenly have to work on the computer, or leave the apartment. It seemed like a million years, since I had come up with the idea of seducing the information out of him. That hadn't worked at all like I planned. I needed to get out of here. I couldn't take it anymore. Cruz was like a drug to my system. I was losing myself. Allowing my heart to grow soft. I wasn't trusting my instincts, the one sending up red flares. I knew better.

    I pulled out the to-go bag Cruz had grabbed from my apartment. At the bottom, I had a few wigs under some hairclips and ties. I had gone through a phase where I wanted to change my hair color and style but couldn't afford a salon. I guess I hadn't really grown out of that phase completely. Sometimes I felt like I wanted to be someone else, like one of my college friends. They would be shocked by my past. I went back and forth trying on different wigs deciding exactly who I wanted to be today. I settled on the dark-blonde bob. It was sassy and sweet. The exact opposite of what I felt like. It reminded me of my bubbly friends from college, the ones that would crumble over a broken nail. They were marshmallows. All of them. It didn't mean I didn't enjoy having friends, but they tended to be superficial. Don't get me wrong. They were still nice. I wouldn't have been friends with them otherwise. But they hadn't had the kind of life experience that shaped those that lived in fear. I slipped on the blonde bob, adding some makeup and a hat. I made sure my outfit was boring, nothing that would catch anyone's attention. My body looked more like a blob in loose-fit yoga pants and a plain t-shirt. Cruz had said someone was watching the apartment. My guess was they were only watching the main stairwell in the front. I had investigated every inch of the apartment that first day, finding all the escape routes. It was a force of habit from growing up with an abusive stepdad. With disguise in place, I crawled out the back bedroom window and slid down the fire escape with my backpack. I had to mail a few Etsy jewelry orders for my clients.

# SANTA FE SEDUCTION

I had been bored silly cooped up in that apartment, so I had finished most of them. I had to make a living after all. But that wasn't the only reason for getting some sun and fresh air. I also wanted to grab Benjie's journal from its hiding spot. I decided it was time to show it to Cruz. Maybe if I shared my secret, he would start sharing his. It was a tactic I hadn't yet tried. Perhaps the gibberish from the journals would mean something to him. He had spent more time with Benjie recently. I had de-coded a few pages of the journal in Tempe using the old code Benjie and I had come up with as kids, but it still didn't make sense. After discovering Benjie's apartment ransacked the first day in town, I had stashed the journal in a locker at the Santa Fe Depot. My brother had entrusted me with the journal for some reason. It had to mean something.

※ ※ ※

The bus stop was across the street from the apartment. I waited by the back of the building until I saw a couple walking their dog. A little Yorkshire Terrier with pink bows.

"Oh, what an adorable dog you have."

"Thank you so much." The woman puffed up, obviously a proud dog parent.

"You wouldn't happen to know where the bus stop is?" I asked. "I'm new to the area."

"Of course." The man said. "It's right across the street. We always walk past it on our way to the park that our Rosie loves."

"Thanks."

I walked with the couple so it would look like we were a group to anyone watching. I asked the woman questions about Rosie, and we chatted back and forth. I learned more about their dog in five minutes than I usually learned about people's kids. I forced myself not to glance around or look nervous when we crossed the street. I bent down to scratch Rosie's ears and thanked the couple again when I got to the bus stop. I stayed at the back of the crowd of people waiting for the bus. I decided to stop at the post office first, then catch another to the depot and back to the apartment. The whole trip shouldn't take too long. I'd be back before Cruz ever knew I was missing. My plan was perfect. Although his voice was in my head warning me, nagging at me to be careful the whole time. Every person I encountered on my trip looked suspicious. I was getting paranoid. Just like Cruz. At least my situational awareness was better. I hadn't used those skills in a very long time. But I guess getting drugged and almost kidnapped would do that to a girl.

## Chapter 20

*Cruz*

"It will be done, Lobo Rojo." I heard one of the goons say to Luís as he backed out of his office.

All of the security guards fresh from Columbia spoke mostly Spanish. And they all called him that. The more frequent use of his nickname made me nervous. It could have also been the sheer number of new people that surrounded him lately. The tension was thick in the air as I helped Ramón gather supplies from the back. He had been surprised but grateful by the gesture. Luís was doing another charity event, so we would be busy tonight. The irony of the situation was not lost on me. The idea that a drug lord with his family name would raise money to help kids get off drugs was ludicrous. The same drugs he made a fortune supplying. I knew it was just a ploy to ingratiate himself with those in high society. He looked like a model citizen, a generous businessman giving back to the community, but it was all just an act. I saw through the lies. I couldn't believe how easily he fooled the public. It made my skin crawl. Staying his employee was almost impossible. But I had a job to do, and I wouldn't give up.

# ZIZI HART

Slipping into the back hallways of the club, I was able to hear more useful information than I usually did as a bartender. No wonder BJ had been able to provide so much intel. He hadn't been high up in the organization. In fact, he had been the opposite. But he had been in the right place at the right time, to overhear things that he passed along to me. In the end, his luck had run out, but I wasn't about to make the same mistakes. I unfolded the list of items we needed from the kitchen, and Ramón took off to find them. I was in the supply closet loading the rest of the list from the shelves onto a cart. Through the thin hidden doorway, I could hear someone entering Luís' office. I didn't recognize the high-pitched whiney voice. The guy gave a yelp and must have been shoved into a chair by the sound of it. I wished I had video in his office, but it was too risky for cameras. Luís' paranoia was already bad enough. I couldn't imagine what he would do if he found something like that. The voices were muffled, but I managed to hear most of the conversation.

The newcomer was doing a job for Luís. He was some kind of computer expert. The guy prattled on about his computer skills, and it sounded like paperwork was exchanged.

"Why did you print this out?"

"I thought you wanted a hard copy." The guy's voice cracked. "It's a transcript of the messages between her and her friends."

There were a few thuds, and groaning. Not a surprise. Luís typically handled business in this manner.

"I don't understand." The guy wheezed. "Didn't you want to know who Mari Miller was messaging and what was said?"

I stopped any pretense of gathering supplies and held my breath.

I heard the screech of Luís' chair, and knew he was trying to intimidate the guy. He had done the same thing to me a few

# SANTA FE SEDUCTION

times. Luís liked that sound. It usually made those sitting in front of his desk jump. He enjoyed seeing fear in others. I imagined the computer geek was pissing himself right about now.

"You cloned her account?"

"Yes sir. And I have the program. I can install it on your laptop."

The geek made another yelp and it was a different more subdued screech. My guess was the geek had been seated in one of the smaller metal chairs that Luís reserved for special occasions.

"You have 15 minutes to install it. I don't expect to hear from you ever again. Got it?"

"Yep. Right away sir. No problem."

The door slammed and I knew Luís had left.

"Eyes on the computer. Geek-boy."

"Uh. My money?"

The goon laughed. "I got it for you. Once you're done."

Then all I heard was a faint clacking of keys. Ramón arrived with the rest of the items, and helped me push the cart back to the front. We worked in silence. I wondered if the kid knew what I was doing in that closet, or if he had learned from experience to keep his mouth shut. While restocking the bar, I went over the conversation in my head. The implications made my heart race. Mari was obviously messaging her friends. Something I had absolutely forbidden her to do. And now Luís was using someone to hack her accounts. He was escalating the search, and using a new method to find her. Employing an outsider was highly irregular. I wondered when it would be safe to get a message to Mari. I had to figure out a way to leave the bar before it was too late. I needed to warn her. No screw the warning. I needed to get her somewhere safe. I devised a plan. I felt slightly bad for making Ramón the scapegoat, but not enough to change my mind. I pulled out the blender, adding a few extra items when he wasn't looking.

## ZIZI HART

"Let's test your skills on some blended drinks."
Ramón bounded over. He was always so eager to learn anything I was willing to teach. It didn't take long before the blender fried with a puff of smoke. It set off the smoke alarms. Luís came out of his office and zeroed in on the blender. I backed away leaving Ramón to explain. He was still busy apologizing to his uncle, when I left the bar. I told Rosa I was grabbing another blender before the bar opened. She would pass along the message if anyone asked.

◆ — ◆ ⋖◆⋗ ◆ — ◆

It took everything I had to keep my car slow as it pulled out of the parking lot, and not peel out. I didn't keep to the speed limit once I hit the freeway. I could kick myself for not providing Mari with a burner phone. I had no way to warn her, so I called Jac.

"Dillon here."
"It's me."
"What happened?" He asked.
"It's BJ's sister, Mari. She's in trouble."
"I thought she was staying at your place."
"She is. But she's been messaging on social media."
"Shit. Didn't you warn her?"
"Of course, I did." I groaned. "You remember when she stopped by your office a few weeks back?"
"Yeah. She looked like she wanted to punch me when I told her I closed her brother's case."
"And you remember how stubborn BJ was?"
"Yep. That guy was like a mule."
"Well, the sister is twice as bad. She doesn't listen. Mari thinks she knows everything. I can't control her."
I swerved around a car. He honked. I gave him the finger.
"Are you in the car?"

## SANTA FE SEDUCTION

"Yeah, I'm driving back to the apartment now. I left the club to run an errand. I won't blow my cover as long as I get back within the hour. I overheard Luís talk to some tech guy. He's got transcripts of her messages, and he's cloning her social media account. Luís is getting close. There's no more time. Can you meet at my place? I need to make sure she's ok."

"What's the plan?"

"I want to come clean. Tell her everything. It's time."

"Do you need me to find a safe house?"

"I don't trust the system right now. There have been too many accidents. And Luís has too many influential friends. Santa Fe isn't safe." I took a deep breath not sure how Jac would react. "I'd like you to take her to mi mamá's."

"Irene's house?"

"Yeah. You got a problem with that?"

"No. Anything. You know that. I'll make sure she's safe."

I nodded my head even though he couldn't see me. "Thanks man. I owe you."

I hung up and called mi mamá. One of my sisters answered the phone.

"Who is this?" Sofía asked.

"What? No hello. Is that how you answer the phone these days?"

"César. It's been forever." I could hear the smile in her voice. "I didn't recognize your number. Mamá's been getting a lot of scam calls."

"Is she there?"

"Hang on."

I heard a muffled yell. "Mamá! Phone call for you. It's César."

I shook my head. The house wasn't that big, and Sofía was a loudmouth.

Mi mamá came on the phone breathing heavy. "Estas bien?"

## ZIZI HART

"I'm fine Mamá. Don't worry. I just need a favor."

"Don't tell me what to do. I worry if I want to." She sputtered. "What's this favor? Are you coming home?" Her voice went up an octave. "Finally. It's been too long. I make arroz con pollo. Sofía will make up spare room."

"Stop Mamá. It's not for me."

"Qué?"

"I'm sending a girl to you, to stay for a while?"

"Dios mío! You get some girl pregnant? Mi hijo descarriado. ¿Qué has hecho?"

"I haven't done anything and she's not pregnant. Calm down. I'm sending a Detective down there with her. You remember Jac. Jac Dillon."

"Jac is such a good boy. He didn't get a girl pregnant, did he?"

I shook my head. "Nobody's pregnant."

Why was she on this pregnancy kick? I knew she wanted grandkids. But damn!

"So why is she staying here?"

"She's in danger. I need you to look after her for a little while. A couple of days. I have to finish my work, then I'll be down for a visit."

"My house is not a hotel. Who is this girl?"

"Her name's Mari." I sighed. Did I want to tell mi mamá the truth? Did I have much of a choice? "She's my girlfriend."

Silence. I must have shocked mi mamá. I had never brought a girl home to meet the family, ever.

She cleared her throat. "Por supuesto!"

"Thanks, Mamá."

She chuckled. "Take care Césarito. Te amo."

"I love you too, Mamá."

✦ — ✦ ⟨◆⟩ ✦ — ✦

# SANTA FE SEDUCTION

I only lived 15 minutes away from the bar, but the way I drove, I made it there in ten. Even with the phone calls, it was the longest drive of my life. I unlocked the apartment and sped through looking for Mari but like I had feared, she wasn't there. She must have grown tired of my silence and left. Was she out there looking for the information I refused to share with her? Had my need for secrecy allowed El Lobo Rojo to get her into his clutches once more? She had slipped through my fingers. I hadn't protected her like I had promised. There was no telling where she would be now. It was too late. I had failed. All the bottled-up anger came out in one sweeping ball of fury. Tables were tipped, walls punched, and Mari's beading supplies knocked over. In minutes, my apartment was trashed, and I collapsed back into the couch. It wouldn't be long before Luís noticed I wasn't there and started asking questions. My excuse would only make sense if I returned back to the bar quickly with a new blender in hand. Any extra time, and Luís would grow suspicious. Of course, if he had her, it would lead back to me anyhow. I had invested nearly 6 months working this job, and I realized I didn't care if it all fell apart. My heart was pounding so hard it felt like my body would explode. All external sounds ceased to exist. I could only hear the thundering in my own chest. I hadn't fathomed how much she meant to me. I never told her. And now, she was gone.

## Chapter 21

*Mari*

I snuck back into the apartment as quietly as I could. Not that I expected anyone to be there. I stared at the mess in confusion. It looked like the place had been ransacked. Was it Luís' people? We're they still after me? Maybe I should have listened to Cruz and all his warnings. Fear gripped me. My chest tightened. I couldn't get enough oxygen. I made my way over to the couch. That's when I saw Cruz. I hadn't seen him at first, half buried in the cushions, unmoving. He looked unconscious. I studied his flawless body for injuries. The only blood I could see were on his hands, the ones covering his perfect face. I rushed to his side and shook him awake. It was probably the worst thing to do if he had a concussion but what did I know. I'd never taken anything past basic biology in school.

"Cruz. Are you ok? Ohmygod. Ohmygod. I don't know what to do." I started to hyperventilate.

His eyes blinked open slowly and he stared. "Mari." He whispered.

He touched my face tentatively, like he wasn't sure I was real. He fingered the locks from my wig and grinned.

"You look good as a blonde."

# ZIZI HART

Before I could utter a word, he grasped the back of my neck and pulled me in for a kiss. I collapsed into him, molding my body to his. The kiss was brutal, demanding. It was unlike any of the others before. There was emotion to it. So much. Almost too much. I lost myself in that one perfect kiss, our tongues twining together. I wanted it to go on forever.

A throat cleared behind me and I jolted. I hadn't heard anyone enter.

It was followed by a deep masculine chuckle.

"I like what you did to your place, César."

"Fuck off Dillon. Can't you see I'm busy?"

Another chuckle.

I tried to move out of this undignified position, with my legs wrapped around Cruz's hips, but he held me in place.

Wait. The guy called him César.

I pushed back, and squirmed in his arms, forcing him to loosen his grip or risk hurting me.

"César?"

His cheeks darkened.

"Your name isn't even Cruz?"

I shoved myself off the couch and stumbled into the stranger. I turned around and my mouth dropped. It was the Detective. The one I had met with at the police station weeks ago, just after Benjie died. What was he doing here?

"You."

He swiped invisible dust from his shoulder. "Me."

I couldn't remember his name.

He held out his hand. "The name's Dillon."

I looked back at Cruz, or rather César. He didn't seem particularly threatened to see a cop in his apartment. Did this Detective Dillon know what Cruz did for a living? The subject I avoided at all costs to speak of, because I was a coward.

I could kick myself for not demanding answers. How well did I really know this man? I didn't even know his real name. I

# SANTA FE SEDUCTION

couldn't think about it any further. I wanted out of there. Anywhere to get away from this conversation.

"I don't want to talk to you. Whatever the hell your name is, just how many secrets have you been keeping?"

César hung his head. At least he had the decency to act guilty. Not sure it was a real emotion. It could have all been an act. I turned toward the bedroom. I needed to get away. Making my way down the hallway, I could feel César's eyes on my back. He quickly caught up to me.

"I don't need you arguing with me right now." César threw me up against the wall. I would have loved this aggressive move in other circumstances, but this was hardly playtime. He was clearly pissed off. And he had no right to be. He had lied. I should be the one that was angry.

"You're in danger. Don't you get that? Luís had your social media account cloned. You've been reaching out to your friends. Like I had warned you not to do." He threw his hands in the air and stomped away.

"Wait just a minute." I chased after him and joined him in the bedroom.

"You don't get to storm away after that. You're the one that hasn't given me any information this whole time."

The look he gave me was devastating. Anguish and hurt. Remorse. Guilt. So many emotions crossed his face. We both glanced at the bedspread. It was still in disarray from an earlier tumble. It would be so easy to get distracted in each other's bodies. That might have been our problem. We had been going at it every spare moment. Talking we weren't good at. Sex. Yeah. That was incredible. I had never had a lover so completely in the moment. His only purpose seemed to be satisfying my every desire, even those I hadn't realized I had. Each time together was better than the last. I didn't see how it was possible. But none of that mattered because I didn't really know the man in front of me.

"I need you to go with Dillon to Albuquerque."

# ZIZI HART

"What?" Oh yeah, I had completely forgotten about the visitor standing in the living room.

"I don't have time to explain."

"You never do."

He flinched, but I didn't care. If Cruz, or César wanted me out of his life, then I would go. I gathered up my stuff and shoved it in my backpack. I found Miles in the living room. He was sitting on César's chest playing with a pile of feathers from the couch. It was absolutely adorable, and I hated César for it. He handed me the kitten. I ignored how gently he placed Miles in my hand and how our fingers lingered.

I turned and walked to the door. Dillon and César whispered to one another, so I stood there feeling uncertain. I snuggled Miles to my cheek, and he gave me a rumbling purr. When the two were done, César approached, and I shook my head. I didn't want to talk to him, but unfortunately needed to tell him one thing before I left.

"Here." I handed him Benjie's journal. "This is the main reason I left the apartment earlier."

César flipped through the pages. "What is this?"

I shrugged. "I was hoping you might know. My brother mailed it to me weeks ago. He asked me to keep it safe, which I did. I had it stored in a locker at the bus station. It has a code that Benjie and I used when we were kids. I deciphered a couple pages, but it's complete nonsense."

"Let me look at that." Detective Dillon reached for the journal.

"BJ sent me something a few weeks back as well. Maybe if we put them together."

"Why would he be sending you anything?" I asked the Detective.

"He was my CI."

"What?"

"BJ was working undercover at the club. Just like César."

# SANTA FE SEDUCTION

My jaw dropped.

"You knew what was going on at the club?"

Dillon nodded. "We knew there was drug trafficking at the club, but we wanted to get the big boss. For that we needed evidence to build a case against him. We also need the supplier. If we could get everyone in the drug ring, we could take down the whole operation. BJ knew there was a large shipment coming in. He contacted me and said he had been keeping track of everything. He had dates, names and addresses. All the contacts, all the way up the chain, including politicians and judges that would bury this investigation, and sweep any arrest under the rug. He thought that deserved a larger check from the Santa Fe PD." He sighed. "The next day he turned up dead."

I couldn't believe what I was hearing. My brother had been a CI. And Cruz, or rather César had been working undercover this whole time.

"Was he murdered?"

"I don't know. Nothing we could prove. And an investigation would have put César at risk."

César didn't say a word. He stood there staring at me. He had told me nothing over this past week, no matter how hard I tried to get him to talk. This man had kept all this from me. Had he felt anything for me? Or had I just been a convenient lay because we were stuck living together? Tears streamed down my cheeks. I didn't have the energy to wipe them away.

"I'm sorry Mari. If I could have told you, I would have."

He went to hug me, and I flinched.

César sighed and took a step back.

I followed Dillon out to his car after he made sure no one was watching. But just in case, I kept my disguise on from earlier. Apparently, Luís had his guys searching everywhere for me. Dillon filled me in on our drive to Albuquerque.

"How long was he undercover?"

"Your brother or César?"

# ZIZI HART

"I guess both."

"Your brother started working at Club Cuervo 13 months ago. A friend of his had gotten him a job as a barback. Then ten months ago, that friend overdosed. That's when I met your brother for the first time. BJ was ready to quit his job at the club, but I asked if he would be willing to help the police. I offered to buy the information. He would report back to me anything illegal he saw happening at the club. BJ decided this was a way for his friend to get justice."

"That sounds like Benjie." I sniffed. "He was loyal. Always a good friend. When he wasn't using."

"After a few months, I realized we needed more eyes and ears. We couldn't use anyone locally. César is an old friend of mine. We went to school together. He's worked undercover for Albuquerque PD for several years. We needed a fresh face to infiltrate the club. His undercover contacts knew him as Cruz Diaz, so he got one of them to vouch for him, and he got the job as a bartender at Club Cuervo."

Cruz was a cop. I kept repeating it in my head over and over. No matter how many times I said it to myself, it still felt wrong. He was a bad boy with an edge. Cruz was the least cop-like person I had ever met. He had passed along drugs to customers with ease. Smooth as silk. That couldn't be allowed, could it? Didn't he have some sort of ethics to uphold that wouldn't allow him to do certain things? Had he fooled the Santa Fe PD? Why was I struggling to see him as a good guy? I had wanted to believe that he cared for me. Was it such a stretch that he cared for others as well, that the bad-guy image he portrayed was fake? I didn't know what to believe anymore. I was still wrapping my head around his name. César didn't fit. Even though I had only known him a short time. I didn't think I would ever be able to see him as anything other than Cruz.

"Did my brother know that Cruz was a cop?"

# SANTA FE SEDUCTION

"No. BJ only met with me. We limited the amount of people knowing about the case. Luís has political contacts. If they knew we were trying to gather information on him, the investigation would be over before it got started. César watched out for BJ; you know. He made sure nothing happened while he was at the club. César would have stepped in, even if it had blown his cover. It hit him hard when BJ died. He was at the club working when it happened."

"So, you both failed protecting my brother!"

My voice was a high shrill sound and Dillon winced.

"Don't blame César. If anyone blame me. If I hadn't asked BJ, he might have still been alive."

"I know my brother. He would have still wanted revenge. You gave him an outlet. A purpose. He probably would have started using that same week if you hadn't given him the job. Why hadn't you told me any of this weeks ago, when we first met?"

"I'm sorry. I couldn't."

After Benjie's death, I had been directed to Detective Dillon's desk at the Santa Fe PD. I might have made a scene at the station. I believe I told him to get off his fat ass and look for my brother's killer. He had been curt with me and told me to watch my attitude. After that brief encounter, I realized the Santa Fe PD would be of no help. They considered his death an accident. Case closed. Dillon especially seemed completely ambivalent. I hadn't been back there since.

"I thought there might have been foul play when your brother passed." He cleared his throat. "I wasn't sure of course. It was just a hunch."

I blinked several times. Tears threatening to fall. So, he assumed, but still did nothing?

"Why didn't you do anything?" I shrieked throwing my hands in the air.

Dillon rubbed a hand on the back of his neck. "Listen, I'm sorry about your brother, but like I said before, we didn't have proof. Investigating could have disrupted the whole operation. A lot of man hours were put into this. Jumping the gun early, trying to make an arrest without enough evidence wouldn't bring your brother back. BJ wanted to get El Lobo Rojo, for his friend. BJ died doing just that, whether it was an overdose or not."

    I was silent for the rest of the drive. Dillon jumped off and on the freeway a few times. He explained it was to double check we weren't being followed. I think he was trying to get me to say something. I held Miles and tried to figure out who I was really mad at. I tended to go towards anger first. Benjie, Dillon, and César all made my list for various reasons, but I probably should be blaming Luís Lorenzo, the drug lord better known as El Lobo Rojo. He was the one that really deserved my rage. We pulled into the circular driveway of an adobe house and Dillon shut off the car.

    "Where are we?"

    "Albuquerque. This is César's mother's house."

    What a way to meet the family.

    "This won't be awkward as hell." I stepped out of the vehicle and slammed the door, carefully tucking Miles into my coat. He got nervous around new people.

    Three women stood in the entryway, lit up by the porchlight. They all had dark hair and caramel skin just like César. One of the women was older, I'm guessing the mother. She stood slightly in front of the others.

    "Welcome to my home, Mari." She fussed with her apron smoothing it out. "My name is Irene Ramirez. These are my daughters Sofía and Gabriela." She gestured to each of her girls in turn. "Come on in. Dinner's ready."

    Sofía had this devoted sappy expression on her face. Her eyes were glued onto Detective Dillon. I glanced back at him. I guess he was good-looking in that clean-cut boy next door kind of way. He was certainly tall, maybe a few inches shy of six and a

# SANTA FE SEDUCTION

half feet. Since I had labeled him an asshole that first day I met him, it was hard seeing him as anything else.

"Are you staying Jac?" She cleared her throat. "Mamá has made plenty."

He grinned. "How can I refuse Irene's cooking?"

Sofía smiled and took Jac's arm and escorted him inside. The other two women stared at me. Miles peeked from the lapel of my jacket and meowed.

"I hope it's ok that I have a kitten. I rescued him from a gas station a few weeks ago. He's a little skittish."

Irene growled. "César say girlfriend. He said nothing about some mangy stray."

"Aww." Gabriela cooed. "He's so cute. Mamá, please let him stay."

"Fine." Irene huffed. "Dinner's getting cold."

The mother shooed me inside like she was directing traffic. I was in shock over that one word. César had told his mother I was his girlfriend. I repeated that over and over to myself. Maybe he didn't want to get rid of me after all. He could have put me up anywhere. A safehouse. A hotel. Why had he chosen his family's home? That had to mean something. I had to mean something to him. I gave his mother and sister a beautiful smile and graciously accepted their hospitality.

## Chapter 22

*Cruz*

I made it back to the club with the new blender. Luís was still in his office. Rosa winked at me when I walked in. I slapped her ass and she rolled her eyes at me but said nothing. We were still playing that we were a couple. Ramón was busy polishing the bar. Relief flooded his face when he saw me.

"Thanks for picking up a new one. I'm such a güevón."

I felt bad for the kid, especially since it wasn't his fault. I had been the one to sabotage the appliance for an excuse to leave.

"No big deal. That's how you learn."

He took the blender out of the box and started washing all the pieces.

"You did a great job on the bar."

It gleamed in the overhead light.

"My uncle made me do it."

I bet he had really ripped into his nephew. El Lobo Rojo might have killed anyone else for causing the fire alarm to go off and disrupt whatever plans he had in that psychotic mind of his. We went through the prep list, and Ramón had everything in place for this evening. The kitchen was busy creating dishes that would be served for another charity event to help those with addictions.

# ZIZI HART

It grated on my nerves. He had been selling that image of himself for months, fake concern and outrage for the drug trafficking problem in the community. El Lobo Rojo should have been an actor. He played his part brilliantly. Even I might have believed him, if I hadn't been in the know. It frustrated me that no one seemed to see through his disguise. I was sick of everyone praising him for his generosity. Did the politicians really believe, or were they just being paid to look the other way? I stopped getting things set up long enough to glance at my phone. Jac texted to let me know they had made it safely to mi Mamá's. I breathed a sigh of relief. I could cross one of the many worries off my list. Now to just stay alive and out of El Lobo Rojo's way long enough for the shipment to arrive. Then it would all be over. I could take some time off. Somewhere tropical, with Mari by my side. If I could convince her to join me. The thought of Mari in a bikini made me grin. That image would get me through the night.

◆ — ◆ ⟪◆⟫ ◆ — ◆

Luís signaled for me to send over a special bottle of Patrón. The coaster held pills that he planned to share with his friends. I wasn't sure what was in the baggies. Bruno had personally added them to the coaster marked for Luís. I handed the bottle service to Rosa and she delivered it to the men. The women surrounding them looked like minors. They had on short dresses, stilettos and way too much makeup, but their eyes were a little too wide with inexperience. And I couldn't do a damn thing about it. The group went to the back toward the private rooms. Young, innocent girls hanging all over men twice to three times their age. The whole thing made me sick.

Rosa came back to the bar with a snarl.

"Those gringos are pigs."

"What did they say?"

# SANTA FE SEDUCTION

"One invited me to a threesome with one of those children." She huffed. "As if I'd ever stoop so low."

"You forget you're supposed to be screwing me."

"Don't remind me." She rolled her eyes.

"You're going to hate me for asking."

"Go on."

"Any chance you can go back there in a bit to make sure the girls are ok?"

Normally I wouldn't ask, but I wasn't sure I could let this one go. I had to do something.

"You becoming a superhero in your spare time?"

I gave her a wicked grin.

"I see, you've just grown incredibly stupid."

"You'd probably need to go check on their drink orders at some point, right?"

"Sorry my mistake. You think I'm stupid."

"You're his cousin. Doesn't that grant you some leeway."

"Luís has loads of cousins. So many in fact, that he would barely bat an eyelash to lose one." She sighed. "Plus, I'm a woman. That means I'm beneath him. I barely register on the importance scale."

"So, you're invisible. That's an advantage."

"Do you get off on these mind games?"

"Maybe."

"Just because I stuck my neck out for your little friend doesn't mean I'm going to do that for just anyone."

Bruno was watching our exchange with interest.

"Please." I whispered in her ear.

It looked like I was flirting to anyone watching.

"You aren't going to let this one go."

My smile slipped away. "No."

Rosa stared at me. I know she was working out my angle. She was smart. Otherwise, she wouldn't still be alive. The Lorenzo family had no problem culling the herd when necessary.

"You owe me," She wagged her finger in my direction., "Whenever I ask. Whatever I say." Rosa demanded.

I nodded, wondering what she'd come up with.

Rosa grabbed her tray and spun on her heels.

---

A short while later, Rosa went back to the private room. I'm assuming she'd go under the pretense of asking if they needed anything from the bar. Luís had already left the back room to attend other guests.

Rosa navigated a path in-between those on the dance floor and handed me a slip of paper. She normally didn't write down drink orders, she'd just yell them in my ear. She was not a quiet woman.

The note said, 'The pills are roofies. One of the girls refused to take them and is crying in a corner. The rest are getting molested by the gringos.'

"We need a distraction."

"Yeah, but what?"

I thought about the fire alarm from this afternoon, but I wasn't about to burn up another blender, or throw Ramón under the bus. We needed something else.

I noticed some kids heading outside to smoke. They already had the cigarettes in their mouths. Trying to look cool.

"I've got it."

I bummed a smoke from one of the kids and ran to the bathroom. I lit the cigarette. Gave a few puffs to get it going, then set it on the toilet paper roll holder in the stall. I locked the stall and walked out. The smoke caused the alarm to blare, and we ushered people out of the club. I went toward the private rooms to escort the gentleman out. In the chaos, the girls were separated from the men with a little help from me. I handed the crying girl

# SANTA FE SEDUCTION

a wad of cash and told her to grab her friends and go home. She nodded her head repeatedly and shoved her friends out a side door.

After completing my rounds to make sure that everyone was outside the club safely, I looked for the girls, but they were no longer in the parking lot. The men I had rescued from the private room were desperately searching the crowd. The girls had probably caught one of the earlier taxis. Many of the guests were leaving in droves.

Luís was pacing back and forth. It looked like he was going to blow a gasket, but people were watching. He shook out his shoulders and focused on the firetruck that had just arrived. It didn't take long before the firemen came back out. They handed Luís the cigarette that had started the whole thing. His eyes darkened as he crushed it in his palm. El Lobo Rojo looked ready to howl.

# Chapter 23

*Mari*

The aroma of peppers, garlic, and onion overwhelmed my senses as I walked through Irene's front door. I hadn't been hungry, but I was suddenly starved. It had been so long since I had a home cooked meal. I wasn't the best cook, so I tended to eat fast-food or microwave dinners. Even Miles poked his head out and sniffed his little nose in the air. His little rumble of a purr vibrated my chest and put me at ease. It smelled like home. One filled with love and laughter wrapped in a cocoon of spices and herbs. The exact opposite of where I had grown up.

"Can I hold your kitten?" Gabriela asked.

"He doesn't really like people all that much."

"Maybe he just needs to get to know me." She smiled.

Miles cautiously watched her as she talked softly. He tilted his head. When she reached out to him, he allowed her to rub under his chin. His eyes closed in bliss. She seemed to have the magic touch. He was willing to sniff her hand, and then he was passed to her. He still watched me, but he seemed content with Gabriel. I was amazed.

"Let me grab a few things for him." She took off running to what I assumed was the garage. "He meowed, but held onto her as she flew through the house talking to him softly in Spanish.

"Gabriela! Get back here for dinner." Irene yelled. "Esa chica loca."

A few minutes later she returned with a box of sand that she threw in the bathroom, along with a small basket of blankets, and a cup of water.

"You aren't using my good blankets, are you?"

"Mamá. I can't give the little guy dirty old rags. We want him to be comfortable. He's our guest."

"Gato sarnoso. Un invitado. Es ridículo."

"Stop calling him mangy Mamá." Gabriela set him on the floor in the basket. "He's beautiful."

"Hmph." Irene grunted.

"Wash your hands and help me bring the food to the table. Everyone, take a seat."

In minutes the meal was served. Miles meandered under the table, circling everyone's legs, looking for scraps. Gabriela kept sneaking him small pieces of chicken.

"So, how do you know our Césarito?" Irene asked.

"We met twelve days ago."

"And he already calls you, his girlfriend?" Sofía asked.

I shrugged. This situation was all new to me.

"I drove from Tempe to Santa Fe to find out how my brother Benjie died. César worked with him at the club."

Irene crossed herself. "Lo siento. A brother. That's awful. How did he pass?"

"Accidental drug overdose was the official report." I looked at Detective Dillon. "But I'm not sure."

"What club did they work at?" Sofía asked.

"Club Cuervo."

"Where he works undercover for the police."

"What's this?" Irene screeched.

# SANTA FE SEDUCTION

I looked at Detective Dillon and he shook his head.

"Maybe I shouldn't have said anything." I grimaced. How was I supposed to know César hadn't told his family?

"Jac Dillon, are you keeping things from me?" Irene scolded.

He sighed. "You know César works for the police. We borrowed him for an assignment in Santa Fe."

"That's why he keeps missing Sunday lunch!" Irene shook her finger at Jac.

"It will be over in a few days. I promise. He'll make it this Sunday, Mrs. R."

"He better."

---

After the huge dinner, and baked apple empanadas for dessert, we went into the living room where Irene was serving coffee.

Gabriela had already found a spot on the sofa with Miles contently purring on her lap. He had clearly found a kindred spirit.

"Would you like some carajillo, Mari?"

I peered at the liquid in the cup.

"What is it exactly?"

"It's coffee and Licor Cuarenta y Tres."

I could definitely use some alcohol about now. "Yes, please."

I took a sip and my eyes rolled back and I sighed. The citrus and vanilla mixed with the coffee. That hit the spot. "Mmm. Wonderful. Actually, the whole meal was delicious. Thank you so much."

"De nada."

I took a seat, settling on the couch with Gabriela and Miles.

"Storytime." Gabriela grinned.

"Who should it be about?" Irene asked.
"Who's not here?" Sofía asked.
"César, it is."
"Let's see. Well at sixteen he had a lot of admirers." Sofía laughed. "Mamá had to beat them off with a stick."
Irene chuckled. "He was just like his father."
"Papa was very good looking." Gabriela nodded.
Sofía handed me a family picture from the fireplace.
It was César as a little boy standing between his mother and father. He had the same grin and mischievous glint in his eye. Same long lashes and thick unruly hair. The father looked just like César did now.
"This was before Gabriela and I were born. César was always too beautiful for his own good."
"I'm telling your brother you said that." Jac said.
"It's the truth." Sofía quipped. "Both of you had plenty of admirers."
Jac's cheeks turned pink.
"I was nothing like your brother."
"Mi Césarito was a heartbreaker." Irene shrugged. "But maybe that was because he hadn't met the right one." She looked at me with hope in her eyes.
I squirmed under her scrutiny.
"He must have invited a lot of girls to meet the family. Didn't you like any of his girlfriends through the years?" I asked.
Sofía laughed. A loud chuckle. Irene, Gabriela and Jac joined her. Tears streamed down their faces they were laughing so hard.
"Girls showed up on the doorstep from time to time in the early years, but he has never invited someone home." Irene grinned. "That is until you came along."
That gave me a little thrill, despite the circumstances.
"Well, I'm heading to bed." Irene yawned. "Sofía, can you show Mari where she'll be sleeping tonight?"

"Yes, Mamá."

Irene gave me a giant hug, and it was so warm and wonderful that I couldn't help but sigh. I hadn't been hugged like that in years.

"Goodnight Mari. I'll see you in the morning. I'll make a big breakfast. We need to add some meat on those bones. You're liable to blow away before César can rescue you from his Familia loco."

---

After Irene left the room, Sofía snuggled closer to the Detective's side on the loveseat. Gabriela wasn't paying much attention. She was playing with Miles. I thought it might be the signal to make myself scarce. I got up from the couch.

Dillon cleared his throat. "I need to go over a few things with Mari. Police business."

Sofía tilted her head and scrutinized the two of us.

"Fine." She didn't sound fine at all. In fact, Sofía sounded pissed off.

"I'll clear off the dining room table. You can set up in there."

"If you guys need some time," I shrugged, "I don't mind. Dillon and I can talk in the morning."

Sofía rolled in her lips and her eyes brightened. Yeah, maybe I did it to score some points with César's sister. She clearly had a thing for Detective Dillon.

He shook his head. "No. It has to be tonight." Dillon turned to Sofía. "This is important."

"Of course." She sighed.

Dillon went to his car and brought back several files. He spread them out on the table along with the journal and a letter from Benjie. I started to tear up and gave a little sob. Sofía grabbed a box of tissues and plopped them in front of me with concern.

# ZIZI HART

Dillon slid me a second envelope with my name on it. "It was inside the envelope addressed to me" He cleared his throat. "I read it."

I couldn't seem to muster up any anger. I was so grateful to have one last message from my brother. A tear rolled down my cheek and I let out a deep breath. I wiped the tear away with my palm and gathered my courage, carefully opening the envelope and slipping out the single sheet of paper. I recognized his messy handwriting instantly. A sob burst free as I read the letter in silence.

*Mari,*
*If you are reading this, then I'm gone. Know that I love you. I've spent so much time trying to fix past mistakes. Even if I didn't make it out, I have no regrets. I'm sorry to pull you into this world. My only hope is that you find in New Mexico the same thing I did. It's a place for new beginnings. I started over here and so can you. Release all that pain, I know is still buried within. Each defeat makes us stronger. And you're the strongest person I know.*
*All my love,*
*Benjie*

After the tears stopped, I took a tissue and blew my nose. "Sorry. I'm not usually so weepy."

"It's ok." Sofia patted my hand. "I'll let the two of you do what you need to." She left the room giving us privacy.

"If you can't do this." Dillon hesitated.

"Just give me a minute." I took a deep breath. "And I'll be fine."

I opened up the journal. He slid a pad of paper and pen.

"Benjie came up with a cipher when we were young. He was super smart and had always loved puzzles. We would pass each other messages that the adults couldn't understand. It gave us an outlet when things got bad. It's an alpha substitution starting

# SANTA FE SEDUCTION

with J, but we also cross off every 11$^{th}$ letter. The numbers have a different code. You just add 3."

I wrote down a translation of the first page.

"See," I showed Dillon sliding the pad to him. "It still doesn't make any sense."

He pulled out Benjie's letter. The one addressed to him. It had a strange grid with instructions.

"Your brother sent me this. I just didn't know what he meant when he said put them together." He pointed at the journal. "Not until you showed me this."

Dillon translated the page with the grid cipher. It looked like names and numbers, addresses and dates. I wasn't a hundred percent sure. It must have meant something to Dillon because he grinned.

"What does this mean?" I asked.

"It means we have a lot of work to do."

I spent the next several hours translating the pages with Benjie's code. Dillon would then add the grid cipher to translate it further. We had stacks of papers when we were done. The coffee and cookies that Sofía had been supplying us was no longer sufficient to keep me awake. I was fading fast.

"Why don't you show Mari the spare bedroom?"

"She's not a night owl."

"I resent that." I said, but I grinned at both of them.

The adrenaline had worn off long ago. My nerves were frayed and my emotions raw. Sofía escorted me to the bedroom, and before I knew it, the world tumbled around me as I drifted off. I wondered if I would ever learn what really happened to my brother. Did I really want to know? Maybe it was better not to. Like Dillon said on our drive to Albuquerque, nothing would bring him back.

## Chapter 24

*Cruz (César)*

I collapsed onto my couch when I got back to my apartment. Another breakfast burrito from the slowest fast-food joint in the world. I woofed it down in seconds. My phone rang. It was Jac.

"What's up?"

"Just wanted to catch up."

"You still at mi mamá's?"

"Yeah. I'm in a food coma after Irene's Arroz con Pollo."

"You bastard. I just finished off some barely edible breakfast burrito from a drive-thru."

"Them's the breaks working undercover."

"You are getting the home cooked meal I should be having."

"I was probably better company than you would have been."

"Ouch."

"That's what Sofía said at least."

"Of course, she would. Sofía has had a crush on you since high school."

"She's all grown up now."

"I don't like where this conversation is heading."

"Your sister is hot."

"Take that back."

"It's the truth."

"Well, she's off limits."

"Uh huh. Just like Mari was."

"That's different."

I thought about how unethical the whole relationship with Mari was. Explaining that to my superiors was going to be a bitch. I just hoped that I could convince my Lieutenant to cut me some slack. The best way to do that was for this bust to go down without a hitch.

"So how are things going at the club?"

"It's tense. El Lobo Robo has a hair trigger. I'll be glad when this is over. I still haven't gotten the date of the final shipment. But I know it's soon. I don't have to work tonight, so I can do some surveillance, at the club or elsewhere. Once I find out, we'll have to move quickly."

"Well, I have some good news. That's why I'm still here at your mom's in the middle of the night."

"Yeah."

"I've been working with Mari on her brother's journal. She's been helping me decipher it. With the note BJ sent me, things started making sense. He has names, addresses, shipments, and dates. This journal is going to be vital evidence. It even had details on that big shipment. It's due to arrive Saturday night."

"No fucking way. That's awesome."

"Yep. There is a warehouse district in Santa Fe. That's where the trucks are coming in at 3am."

"Do you need me there?"

"No. I'm handling it. I'm meeting with DEA later this morning. You just keep your cover. Club Cuervo will be closed permanently on Sunday. You're almost out. Just two more days. I'm working on a warrant for the club and Luís' residence."

# SANTA FE SEDUCTION

"You don't think that will raise red flags with his influential friends?"

"BJ identified those same friends in his journal. The judge I'm going to for the search warrants is straight. We've got proof. Everyone is going down. We are going to have them all spinning. They will be so worried about themselves; they won't have time to help Luís."

I hoped Dillon was right. But I knew from experience, it never went down as smoothly as you thought it would.

"He's got a lot more thugs from Columbia in town. Do you have the manpower?"

"Trust me."

"Final last words. Just be careful."

"You too."

◆ —— ◆ ⋖═◈═⋗ ◆ —— ◆

I was too wired to go to sleep. Thinking that in less than 48 hours it would all be over. I started writing down all the names from the club that we would have to bring in for questioning, and those involved in the drug trafficking. I made a note on those that had the potential to be flipped. Rosa was at the top. She hated her cousin. I don't think she'd mind sending him to jail. But what would her family think back in Columbia? If she testified, her life could be in danger. She would definitely never be able to return back home. I wasn't sure about Ramón. He was young and impressionable, but he had witnessed his uncle lose it on more than one occasion. He was a loyal Lorenzo, but his uncle may have pushed him too far. He had limited involvement with the drug operation at the club, but that didn't mean he wouldn't be arrested. Dillon had said they didn't care about the small players. They wanted the big dog, El Lobo Rojo.

My mind drifted to Mari at mi mamá's place. She was probably overwhelmed. Mi Familia was a lot to take in. They were loud and intrusive. She would be interrogated about our relationship, and who knows what they were sharing with her. My sisters should have majored in gossip. It was a skill they excelled in.

My phone rang. It was Rosa. It was nearly four in the morning.

"Shouldn't you be in bed?"

"Are you offering?"

I paused. The only reason she would say that was if someone was listening.

"Always."

She laughed, it was deep and sultry and I knew it was fake.

"You're insatiable Cruz."

"No arguments here."

"I wanted to see if we could meet Saturday before work."

Fuck. This was a set up.

"Sure. What time?"

"Maybe 1 o'clock. There's a restaurant around the corner from the club, Nacho Daddy. We can have lunch before our shift."

"You don't want me to maybe meet at your place instead?" I asked.

Another sultry laugh.

"I know exactly what would happen if you came over. Keep it in your pants pendejo."

"Your loss."

"Uh huh."

"I'll see you tomorrow at 1."

"See you then."

I sighed. I'd have to call Dillon again. Someone must have witnessed me say or do something suspicious. I knew Bruno had been watching the conversation between Rosa and myself last night at the club, but he shouldn't have been able to hear anything. Or he could have seen me dive into the bathroom to light the cigarette. Or direct the girls away from those sleazy men at the

## SANTA FE SEDUCTION

club. It could have been any number of things. It meant I was being watched. Closely.

Dillon answered on the second ring.

"Hey."

"My cover might be blown."

"How did you manage that in the last hour?"

"I don't know. I got a call from Rosa. Someone was listening in. My guess, it was Luís. She wants to meet me at 1 o'clock tomorrow for lunch before our shift. I need someone there watching."

"Text me the address. I'll have someone there. Just give the signal if you need to be pulled."

"Are you going to the club tonight?"

"Not sure. I don't have to work. It would probably look fishy. I don't usually go in if I have the night off."

"You gonna drive out to your mom's?"

"No way man. And risk being followed? Not gonna take a chance. I'll probably just lay low at my place."

I heard Sofía talking softly in the background.

"What is my sister doing up this late?"

Dillon chuckled. "It's not what you think. Sofía is supplying me with coffee and sweets while I schedule the operation from your dining room table."

"Is she behaving?"

"As well as can be expected."

I snorted. I couldn't help it. My sister was a wild one. She didn't have a good track record with men. Her latest ex was in prison. As much as I didn't want to think of my best friend and my sister. She could do a lot worse. And already had.

"I'll be in touch." I hung up.

I pulled out my supply of weapons and placed them on the bed, trying to decide how I could strap them under my club wear. I was afraid I was going to need them all for what awaited me.

## Chapter 25

*Mari*

I woke to the sounds of women laughing. The Ramirez family was in the kitchen. Irene was at the stove making breakfast, and Sofía and Gabriela were at the table.

"Ah, Mari. Buenos Dias."

Irene handed me a plate of huevos rancheros. Gabriela passed the tortillas and Sofía slid over the bowl of salsa.

"Have something to eat before you blow away."

"Mamá. Stop giving her such a hard time." Gabriela said.

"We decided to make tamales for Sunday lunch. Have you ever made them?" Sofía asked.

"No. My cooking skills are abysmal."

"Then we'll have to fix that. Mi Césarito has an appetite. He needs a wife that can cook."

A wife? I had just met her son. I liked him. Really liked him. But marriage?

"You're scaring her Mamá." Sofía shook her head. "Just look how her eyes are bulging."

Sofía patted my hand. "Don't worry. Mamá wants all of us to get married and settled down. This is how she does it. We show interest in someone, and she's already planned the wedding, and the names for all the babies."

"I haven't come up with baby names yet."

"Mamá, you have a baby name book next to all your cookbooks."

"So?"

"Arrgh." Sofía threw up her hands.

When Irene pulled a list from the baby book and handed it to me, I was ready to bolt. I read the list. It wasn't names. It was a recipe.

"We start with slow cooking the meats today. Tomorrow all day we make the tamales." Irene said. "You help. It will be fun."

"Ok."

"You've just agreed to hard labor." Gabriela grinned.

"Sofía already picked up all the supplies this morning."

"Didn't you stay up late with Dillon?" I asked.

"Oh ho." Gabriela jibed. "Big sis was getting some with Jac."

"It wasn't like that. He was a perfect gentleman."

"No smooches?" Gabriela asked.

"No." Sofía said, her shoulders slumping.

"Well, he had a lot on his mind. Dillon and César are trying to take down a drug lord."

"What is this about drugs?"

"You know he works undercover in Narcotics, right?"

"We know he is Policia."

I kept forgetting that César did not like to share, apparently that extended to his family.

My head dropped. "Well, I guess the cat's out of the bag."

"What cat? Miles is in his basket." Irene pointed.

The cat tilted his head when he heard his name.

"Sorry. It's just an expression."

"So, how did you and César meet?" Sofía asked.

# SANTA FE SEDUCTION

I sighed, grateful for the change or subject.

"Well, speaking of cats. Miles is the reason."

"How do you mean?"

"I found him at this gas station on my drive from Tempe. My heart went out to the little guy. He was scared and alone, hungry and dirty."

I went through the whole ordeal of how I found him by the gas tanks and my exploits running around in the garage trying to catch him.

"Oh." Gabriela picked up Miles from his basket and covered him with kisses. "Poor Miles."

Even Irene, César's tough mom had tears in her eyes.

"I rescued him and drove to Santa Fe. He didn't want to stay in the box, and at the end of my long trip, when I was exhausted, waiting at a fast-food joint in the drive through at 3am, he got under the pedals. And I rolled into César's car."

Sofía's eyes widened. "César loves his car."

"Oh, I know." I nodded. "He started yelling at me and wouldn't let me explain." I threw my hands in the air remembering how mad I had been at the time. "He was being such a jerk, until I agreed to give him my phone number for the repairs."

They all looked at one another and started laughing.

"He was hitting on you." Sofía chuckled.

"Really?" I asked. "When we first met, I thought he hated me."

"He would have asked for your insurance information if that's all he wanted."

I guess I never really thought of it that way.

"So, you think he liked me from the beginning?"

"Definitely." Gabriela agreed. "And he really likes you now."

"More than likes." Sofía snickered. "César wouldn't bring just anyone home."

## ZIZI HART

"Mi Césarito wants our approval."
I gulped. These women were wonderful, but they could make or break our relationship.
"Mamá, you're scaring her again."

---

Over the next two days, I learned every detail of the tamale making process, as well as anything and everything I could ever want to know about César and his family. Five minutes with the Ramirez women yielded more information than all the time I spent with César trying to get him to talk. On Friday, we slow cooked the meats in huge pots filled with pork, chicken and spices.
"It looks like we are making enough for an army."
"Trust me. There is never enough. I'm like the pied piper with mi tamales." Irene winked. "One whiff, and suddenly the neighbors have excuses to stop by."

---

On Saturday, we shredded the meat and mixed the chili sauce.
"Es muy importante. The secret is in the sauce." Irene said as she carefully stirred the pot and added more spices. "This is a highly coveted Ramirez family recipe. If anyone from the Alonzo Familia asks, you know nunca."
"Don't mind Mamá." Sofía said. "Senora Alonzo and Mamá compete in our church's annual tamale contest, and they are always at each other's throats."
"It's for charity, Mamá." Gabriela shook her head. "You both forget that."
"That mujer said our family recipe is mierda. She wouldn't know a good chili to save her life."

## SANTA FE SEDUCTION

"Let it go, Mamá," Sofía rolled her eyes. "They are both locas."

I put the corn husks in a large bowl of warm water and joined Irene and Gabriela in the living room for a coffee break. Sofía was still mixing up dough in the kitchen.

"My husband died when the kids were young." Irene sighed. "Raising three kids by myself was tough. So many times, I wished my Rafael could have seen them grown up." She gave a little sob. "He would have been so proud."

"Don't cry, Mamá."

"Césarito is so much like his father." Irene dabbed her eyes with a tissue. "He is quite... Um, what's the word in ingles? Virile?"

My eyes widened, and my mouth dropped. This was not the conversation I wanted to be having with his mother.

"If Rafael hadn't died so soon, I would have had a dozen children. All he had to do was look at me and I'd get pregnant."

Sofía entered the living room to my expression of shock.

"Mamá, what did you say to Mari? She looks ready to faint."

Sofía went back into the kitchen and returned with a glass of water.

I drank it down desperate for another topic.

Luckily it was time to start making the tamales.

We went back into the kitchen and set up an assembly line now that everything was prepped. Sofía was in charge of spreading the dough onto the husks. I scooped the filling into the middle. Gabriela folded the husks sealing the edges and Irene placed them into the steam basket. In between batches as we waited for the tamales to simmer and steam, we gossiped and laughed. César's sisters were hilarious. Flamboyant and fun. Irene told family stories, and I felt like I was part of something bigger than myself. As awkward as I thought this stay would be, they made me feel welcome and wanted.

# ZIZI HART

"I want to hear more stories about César. What was he like growing up?" I asked.

"Jac and Césarito were always getting into trouble as kids. Both would protect the smaller kids from bullies in the neighborhood. Jac of course, was always big for his age. So, he intimidated just standing there. Césarito was small, but scrappy. He was strong and smart. He got a reputation for righting wrongs."

"And then in high school he got a different reputation." Sofía's eyes twinkled. "With the girls."

Irene nodded. "Like I said. Just like his papa."

"He was a scoundrel. That's for sure."

I smiled. "It's his face. He's so beautiful, I can barely stand it."

"I'm surprised he didn't wind up with a broken nose, or scars." Sofía shook her head. "He got into fist fights all the time. He was relentless with my boyfriends. Somehow, he always avoided getting hit in the face. My boyfriends, not so much. They had broken noses, black eyes, and busted lips.

"That's a typical big brother thing." Irene said. "Trying to protect his sisters."

"How come he didn't do it with me?" Gabriela asked.

"By then, all the local guys knew better than to touch a Ramirez girl." Sofía scoffed. "Your boyfriends were too afraid to hold your hand, let alone kiss you."

"I never had to go through that. My brother moved out of the house before I started dating." I shrugged. "But I do remember times when Benjie would step in front of my stepfather's fist. He would take the hit that was meant for me."

"Brothers protect. It's what they do." Irene said. "I'm so sorry you had to go through that."

She gave me a hug.

"It's ok." I sighed. "I was used to it. My family wasn't anything like yours. My mom died when I was young, and my

# SANTA FE SEDUCTION

stepfather, well he always treated me and my brother like a burden. He was an alcoholic. And my brother had drug problems. Benjie had been in and out of rehab centers since he was a teen." I shrugged. "Despite all that, he was a pretty good big brother, at least when he was around."

"Oh, you poor thing."

I hadn't wanted them to feel sorry for me. That wasn't my intention. They had shared stories of the past, and I wanted too as well. It was as simple as that.

"When my brother left home at 18, I was so angry. I felt like he had abandoned me. It took me years before I would talk to him. I only reconnected with him about a year ago. He said he was clean. And I believed him. Benjie seemed happy for the first time in so long. He had a steady job, and a purpose. I had no idea his life would be cut short, and I wouldn't get to see him again." I sniffed. "I wish I could have told him how much I loved him one more time."

With tears in her eyes, Sofía grabbed me in a fierce hug and wouldn't let go. Despite not being used to hugs, it felt pretty good.

Irene flipped on the radio. "We need música and Margaritas."

We spent the rest of the day dancing and drinking, in between mass production of the best tamales in el mundo. Irene pulled out photo albums and shared pictures of César growing up. He was so darn cute, it made me wonder just how adorable his kids would be.

So many distractions helped keep my worry at bay. The Ramirez family was loud, but loving. In two short days, I fell in love with the family. I had definitely painted a different picture of César in my head. He wasn't the misogynistic pig that he had portrayed at the club. He was kind and caring, protective and loyal. I realized how I had misjudged him and wanted desperately to tell him. I had lost moments with Benjie because I had been stubborn. I didn't want the same thing to happen with César. All the feelings I had been bottling up came out over way too many Margaritas. I admitted to these amazing women that he had saved me and had done everything he could to protect me despite the cost. I didn't want to let any more opportunities pass me by. I wanted to share all these things with him while I still could.

## Chapter 26

*Cruz/ César*

I walked into Nacho Daddy and immediately saw Rosa in a corner booth. She had on her scantily clad cocktail waitress uniform, but she'd covered it with a trench. Her overblown figure was trying to escape the confines of the coat. I saw relief on her face the moment she saw me. I scanned the restaurant, my heart pounding as I searched for threats. Nothing screamed thugs, or a hit. Everyone appeared normal. Everyday customers and employees. I gave the signal that things were all fine at the window, for whoever Dillon had sent to watch me.

"Thank you for coming Cruz."

"What's this all about?"

"We don't have much time. Luís stopped by my apartment on Thursday night. He wanted to see if I had any influence over you. That's the reason for the call. Is he going to show up here?"

"Maybe." Rosa shrugged. "I needed to invite you to lunch, so I choose the loudest, busiest, most non-Luís place I could think of."

"Why wouldn't he just ask us into his office?" My mind conjured reasons, but none of them encouraging. "What game is he playing?"

"I have no idea. My cousin is loco." Rosa shuddered. "And his insanity is spinning out of control."

"He's still looking for the girl?"

She nodded. "He's obsessed with finding her."

The server came over and I ordered a platter of nachos and a margarita. It looked like Rosa was already on her second drink.

"You should pace yourself. We still have to work tonight."

"Blow me, pendejo. I need it."

I put my hands up in surrender and grinned. It was good to know despite the tension in the air, it hadn't killed Rosa's fighting spirit.

The bell on the restaurant door jingled. I looked over and it was Bruno, one of Luís' goons.

He took a seat at our table, sliding in next to Rosa. Bruno stole a nacho from my plate.

"You don't mind, do you... Cruz?"

He hesitated saying my name. Tension crawled up my spine. Did he know who I really was? Had my alias been burned? Or was I just being paranoid?

"Not at all." I smiled, gritting my teeth. "Help yourself."

Rosa rolled her eyes. "What do you want, Bruno?"

"El Lobo Rojo needs you to run an errand for him after work. A special assignment."

"Both of us?" Rosa asked.

"Yes."

Bruno was watching my reaction, so he didn't catch the worry etched into Rosa's brows for a moment before she smoothed her expression.

Luís had never asked her to do something like that. The thugs, sure. Or maybe me. But not his cousin. She was a woman, and I knew how he felt about them. They were weak. Drug runs or meets were usually reserved for muscle.

"Sorry Bruno, but Cruz and I have plans."

He cracked his knuckles and chuckled.

# SANTA FE SEDUCTION

"It's not a request." He ordered.

Bruno got up and left, but not before grabbing another chip and giving me a smug smile.

"What does this mean?" I asked after glancing to see he was out of ear shot.

Rosa was always good at figuring out her cousin's angle.

"He's waiting for me to screw up. If I don't show, he'll hunt me." Rosa stared into my eyes. "If you don't show, he'll kill me." She took another sip of her margarita with shaky hands. "He loves to play games. He gets off on it. Always has." She pushed the nachos to me. "I'm not hungry."

Everything was screaming that my cover was blown. It was too dangerous. I needed to get out and away, but I couldn't leave Rosa hanging. If I didn't show up to work, she was dead. If I didn't do whatever errand Luís wanted tonight, she was dead. Rosa knew that her life was now in my hands. El Lobo Rojo had me pinned. Her shoulders hunched as she finished off the margarita and signaled for another.

I engulfed her small shaking hands in my own. They were so cold.

"Don't worry. I got this. I won't let anything happen to you."

Tears streamed down her face making the mascara run. Rosa was a hard woman. I had never seen her cry, despite so many times at the club these past months where she should have broken down. A breath whooshed out of her, and she pulled away from my touch. Rosa grabbed a compact from her purse and wiped under her eyes, fixing her makeup. Applying more lipstick, until she was satisfied. Only then did she look at me. Really look at me.

"I always knew." She attempted a smile, but it fell flat. "You're a good guy, despite the tattoos and bad-boy attitude." Rosa laughed. It was broken. "Maybe. In another world. We could have…you know had something."

"Is this your attempt at flirting?" I asked.

She sighed.

"Because you suck at it."

She gave me a grin, and a little chuckle. "Fuck you, Cruz."

There was no heat to her words. I had lightened the mood, which was the point. I hated to see Rosa so serious. It didn't fit her personality.

I went to my car to make a phone call. I needed to call Dillon.

"What's up?"

"I might be blown."

"Shit." Dillon said. "Ok. We're pulling you."

"No."

"What do you mean no?"

"Luís made it clear, it's Rosa's life if I don't show up."

"So what? She's a fucking Lorenzo."

"I can't do it. I can't walk away."

"Fucking hell dude. It's not worth your life."

"All I know is after work, Rosa and I are supposed to run an errand for Luís."

"I'll have someone follow you from the club."

"Yeah. If you could arrange for a tail, that would be great."

"Sure thing. Most of us will be at the warehouse where everything is going down, but I'll have someone follow you."

"Good luck."

"You too."

◆ — ◆ ⬳◆⬲ ◆ — ◆

Rosa and I both showed up at the club like it was any other night. Luís was in good spirits. His eyes gleamed when I walked in. He probably assumed I wouldn't show. I nodded as I passed him in the hall, fighting to keep my stance loose when my insides were twisted in knots. El Lobo Rojo took obvious pleasure during the evening having Rosa serve him and his group of thugs. He let

# SANTA FE SEDUCTION

them slap her ass and feel her up when she delivered drinks to their table. Normally Luís would never allow his men to touch her, but tonight was different. It seemed to be an open market for them to do whatever they wanted. He must have given them permission. Or an order. They never would have stepped out of line otherwise.

A smug sneer formed on El Lobo Rojo's lips, as he watched one of his men grab Rosa around the waist and yank her into his lap. Luís turned his gaze to me, daring me to react. Did he want me pissed off? My shoulders bunched. Jaw tight. I knew my eyes were shooting arrows, but I didn't try to mask my fury. I let Luís see the anger boiling within. If she was supposed to be my girl, it was a natural response. Not that I had ever showed jealousy in the past. I didn't date. One-night stands were more my style. Showing any emotion was a risk, but then again, he didn't tolerate weakness. I knew he was toying with us. Rosa came back to the bar frazzled and rattled off the order.

"Don't let them get to you." I said as I poured the beers and shots. "Remember it's all a game."

"He wants me to react."

"Same here." I glanced over at Luís. "He keeps watching. Waiting."

"What should I do?" Rosa asked as she tapped her nails on the bar.

"Luís once told me how much he enjoyed your attitude. He likes how feisty you are."

"I know. But tonight. He's off." She shook her head. "Ok. I'm gonna try something." She glared at Luís and threw her shoulders back.

"Don't do anything stupid."

She turned back and gave me the finger. There was fire in her eyes. It filled me with hope and dread. Two emotions that normally didn't go together, but that was Rosa. She was a hurricane. Unpredictable. Just like her cousin. She flipped her hair back and sauntered over to the table with the drink order. The one thug who had forced her onto his lap tried again. She slapped his hand away with the tray and poured the drink on his head. Rosa didn't make it look like an accident. It was deliberate and slow. She wasn't looking at the thug when she did it. Rosa stared at her cousin.

Luís grinned. They exchanged words.

The thug got up and stormed away, shaking out his hair.

Luís laughed. A deep rumbling sound that sent shivers down my spine. His enjoyment usually resulted in other's suffering. Luckily whatever Rosa had said, seemed to reset things.

She came back to the bar with a bounce in her step.

"It's handled."

I blew out the breath I had been holding.

---

A few businessmen showed up and Luís was pulled away for a meeting in his office. Either he had lost interest or was too busy to continue his game.

I breathed a sigh of relief. The club was still filled with thugs, associates from Columbia, but not being in his immediate sights gave me a momentary reprieve. There was no charity event this evening, so it was just the normal Saturday crowd. We were busy, but it was manageable. Ramón was visibly nervous, but he wouldn't talk. He broke so many glasses, I sent him in the back to run supplies and nothing else. I didn't need anything to aggravate Luís. He could so easily snap. The rest of the night flew by.

When two o'clock rolled around and I gave the final call, instead of being exhausted my adrenaline spiked. We closed up and Rosa and I were called into Luís' office. I prepared myself for all possible contingencies however horrific they might be. Bruno searched me before I walked in. He took the gun from my holster and slipped out the clip with a grin. My knives came next. At least he missed the hidden one in my belt. Rosa was searched as well. She sneered at Bruno as he slid his hands all over her. Taking his time. He was clearly enjoying his job.

"The boss wants to make sure you aren't carrying anything. He knows you, Rosa."

He said her name rolling the R like it was a candy he wanted to savor in his mouth.

"Like I could hide anything in this scrap of clothing he calls a uniform."

Bruno removed a bodice dagger from between her breasts and smirked.

As we were shoved into the office, I noticed Ramón standing by Luís's side. His eyes darted between Rosa, me, and the several Columbian thugs that stood in the room. I counted eight, not including José, Bruno and Luís. The room felt cramped even though I knew his office was huge. The muscle seemed to take up all the space, leaving little left for anyone else. My shoulders tightened. There was no escape. The only positive thing I could think of was at least we weren't standing on plastic.

"All here?" Luís said. "Very good." He slid some paperwork into a drawer and locked it. "I need everyone with me tonight. We need to sort out some things." His grin was a feral baring of teeth.

He gave a signal and the thugs surrounded us, shoving our hands behind our backs. Our wrists were zip-tied, and our mouths duct taped. We put up a fight, but it was no use. There was too many of them. I got in a few jabs and a kick. Rosa nailed a guy with an elbow. At least a few of them were bloody when they dragged us out back and threw us into a van. They left our feet unbound, so we could greet death standing. I had no illusion on his plans for us. Luís' eyes had filled with amusement as he watched everything play out. I knew he enjoyed the chaos. It would disappoint him to kill us too quickly. Our only saving grace. Although once he got the information he needed, we were

# ZIZI HART

dead. I knew that with certainty. My mind drifted to Mari wondering if I'd ever see again. I forced my thoughts back to the situation at hand. As we drove, I kept checking the doors, paying attention for any opportunity at escape. If one came, I'd take it. We had five goons with us, two in front and three in the back watching us. Only one held a gun. The other two were vigilant. I glanced at my fellow captives. Ramón's eyes were wild with fear. Rosa's were cold. Distant. I tried to keep calm, knowing the boys in blue were following the van. Waiting for their time to move in. But there were no slip ups. The men watching us were good; alert and focused. Before long the vehicle stopped.

The thugs yanked us none too gently from the vehicle and shoved us against the van. We had pulled into a large warehouse. Luís climbed out of a limousine smoking a cigar. The second van pulled in behind him and shut the bay door. The rest of the goons filed out. Everyone from the office was here.

The duct tape was ripped from our mouths. I bit back a curse.

"The three of you are here for one reason." He walked back and forth puffing away. "Something was taken from me. And at least one of you was involved."

"Uncle." Ramón pleaded. "Nunca. I would never steal from you."

Rosa and I stayed silent. We both knew it was Mari he was talking about.

"I could of course shoot you all." He rocked his head back and forth, side to side. "I had considered it. After all, I can't have disobedience. It sends the wrong message. You understand." He used his Glock to nudge Rosa's chin up so she could stare into his eyes.

Ramón fell to his knees. Shaking his head. Sobbing. "Nunca. Nunca. Never. Never. I swear."

"On your feet Ramón." Rosa demanded. Her voice deepened. "You're a Lorenzo."

# SANTA FE SEDUCTION

He sniffed and stared at her, then awkwardly climbed to his feet.

Rosa was clever reminding him they were family. But that left me in the lurch. I tried to slow my racing heart, and wiped all emotion from my face. At this point anything might set him off. I forced my body to relax, loosening my shoulders.

Luís backed up a step to point the gun at each of us in turn. "Two of you are family, and the other a trusted employee."

"How. To. Decide."

We were momentarily saved by the buzz of Luís' phone. He glanced down at his phone.

"They are here." He announced to his men. Luís signaled to Bruno. The majority of the guys proceeded to another docking bay. We watched it open and three large trucks drove into the warehouse.

"If you'll excuse me for a moment." He put the revolver back in its holster, under his jacket. He straightened his cuffs and smoothed out his suit.

A breath hissed out of me. That was way too close. I needed to de-escalate the situation and get us some cover. Someone had closed the second docking bay eliminating another exit. Not that we'd ever get to it in time to escape. I waited until Luís started talking with the drivers. Only two men were left guarding us. Both were new muscle from Columbia. I shared a look with Rosa, trying to convey with my eyes for her to play along. She gave an imperceptible nod, and I fell onto my knees like my legs had given out. I pleaded with the goons to let me go.

"The whole thing's a mistake. I would never do anything against the boss."

Rosa snickered. "This one is no Lorenzo."

"Hey Pablo, can you itch my shoulder?" Rosa asked one of the guards. "With these ties, I just can't reach it."

She wiggled her left shoulder. "This one." It caused her cleavage to bounce.

# ZIZI HART

"Por favor. It's been driving me loca."

In her club uniform, with her hands bound behind her, her Double Ds were more pronounced than ever. She had flirted with all the Columbian guards, and apparently knew quite a few of them when she had lived there. The guard stared at her chest. Leering. Rosa excelled at distraction. It was a skillset I had seen her use on numerous occasions.

I flipped open the hidden knife on the back of my belt, working it against the zip tie until I was almost free.

The other guard slapped his buddy away from Rosa, and slammed me against the van, making me stand in the process. He didn't notice the zip tie now dangled from my wrist. I assessed our situation. Exits. Men. Weapons. The two bay doors were closed. One that the two vans from the club and Luís' limo pulled into. A second door where the three trucks were parked. I counted at least thirty men; ten from the club and twenty or so from the trucks. But there could have been more in the shadows or inside the vehicles. Most were armed. Semi-automatic rifles, a variety of handguns, and a plethora of knives. Raw, hard men with stony expressions. They didn't look military trained, but that didn't mean they wouldn't put up a fight. The warehouse was mostly empty. No racks or machinery. Clearly long abandoned. Some foreclosure from a company gone bust. I stared up at the moon through a broken skylight. Most of the windows were cracked. If things went sideways, and we needed to venture further into the darkness for another exit, there was little hope of cover from gunfire. Just a few pillars that stood between the vehicles and the unknown. Our chances seemed grim. I was just hoping that wherever we were, was the same address that BJ had jotted in his journal weeks before. If Luís had changed the location for the deal, or if the tail from the club had somehow gotten lost, we were fucked.

El Lobo Rojo was yelling at one of the truck drivers. I caught bits and pieces of the conversation. The shipment was short. He was angry they had used a portion to bribe the border control. Luís took out his gun and pointed it at the man. He fired his gun and the man dropped. My muscles tightened, ready to spring into action. An explosion took out one of the bay doors. Flood lights blasted through the opening and several windows, cutting through the thick darkness of the warehouse.

"DEA. You're surrounded."

The voice from the megaphone was drowned out. Guns fired. A staccato from the semi-automatics. Pings as the bullets struck metal pillars and vehicles. The thud of bodies as they fell to the ground. It was a barrage of sound and light. I knocked Rosa to the cement behind the wheel of the van. It didn't offer much protection, but I'd take what I could get. Our two guards were focused on the commotion by the trucks. I relieved the first one of his weapons knocking him unconscious. A sniper from one of the skylights took out the other guard. He dropped dead in front of Ramón. After cutting the zip tie off Rosa's wrists, I turned to Ramón and did the same. The kid was splattered in blood and shaking. Another sniper fired, and Luís took a bullet to his leg. I watched him hobble over to his limousine. But there was no escape. The good guys had the only open bay door blocked. I saw Dillon in the crowd of officers and agents storming the warehouse. SWAT was in front with tactical vests and AR-15s.

I saw the determination in Luís' eyes as he lined up a shot from behind the limo door. I yelled out a warning, but it was too late. He fired and one member of SWAT went down. A volley of bullets fired back at him, but Luís used his driver as a shield.

It didn't take long before they overwhelmed Luís' men. A few tried to run, but they were tackled to the cement. The heavy aroma of burnt smoke and sulfur hung in the air, as I scanned the sea of bodies sprawled across the warehouse floor. Commands were given in Spanish, and those left surrendered.

During the chaos, a stray bullet managed to hit my arm. It was bleeding, but I barely felt a thing. Ramón sprinted to a corner and wrenched out his guts. That kid wasn't cut out for this sort of life. I checked Rosa over, and other than some bumps and bruises, she was unscathed. Dillon was cuffing one of the thugs. His knee in the guy's spine.

"Jac." I yelled, waving him over.

Rosa's mouth dropped.

"You know him," She gasped. "Then you were in on this?"

I had to come clean if I wanted her help. Rosa would make a useful witness. Plus, she deserved to know the truth.

"I was undercover."

"I knew it." She stomped her foot.

One of the DEA agents was arresting Luís. He was screaming bloody murder. Promising his sweet revenge. Swearing in Spanish. Blood dripped down his leg soaking his designer slacks. But just like me, he didn't seem to feel the pain. He glared at me and Rosa as we spoke with Dillon.

"You. I will get you!" He roared, eyes wild, nostrils flaring. His mask of civility shattered. Only the psychotic animal remained.

I wasn't sure exactly who he was referring to, but before he could clarify, someone cold-clocked him. It was a friend of ours, Taz Bennett. A huge Texan, and a US Marshall.

Some reprimand was yelled from the DEA operative running the show.

"What?" Taz shrugged. "He was swearing, and there are ladies present."

He smirked. Taz didn't look remotely sorry as he sauntered toward us.

"How the hell are you, Taz?" Dillon grinned, giving his shoulder a hard slug.

Taz reached out and shook my hand. It had been years since I saw him last.

Rosa just stared at him. He stood a few inches taller than Dillon. The man was built thick like a tree trunk.

"Howdy ma'am." He nodded to Rosa. Concern on his face. "You alright?"

She nodded. Mouth slightly open.

I had never seen Rosa tongue-tied before.

"I don't want Rosa arrested." I told Dillon. "She's been through enough."

"Ramón either." Rosa glanced at me. "I'm calling in my favor."

"What do you think?" I asked. Dillon was the lead detective for the operation with the Santa Fe PD, but since the shipment had crossed several borders, DEA had taken over.

"I'll see what I can do." Dillon nodded.

"What if I…" Rosa glanced between Dillon and myself. "I know things."

"She's a Lorenzo," I said.

Taz tilted his head watching the exchange.

"Luís already thinks I betrayed him. As soon as he lawyers up." She pressed her lips together. "I'm dead."

"We can't have that now, can we? Little lady." Taz said.

She turned her face up to him. He stood a whole head taller than Rosa even in her heels. I think she was trying to work out if he was being condescending or not. I could have explained that it was just Taz. His personality. Ever the Texan gentleman. But she'd realize that soon enough.

Rosa shivered. The adrenaline was finally wearing off.

Taz took off his jacket. He was gentle as he put her arms in. Rosa stood there frowning at him, drowning in his coat. She looked adorable, clearly confused by his effort to console her. She wasn't used to that. Not in her line of work and certainly never by her family.

"Let's get you out of the way." He started walking her over to the line of cars. She stumbled in her heels. He swept her up into his arms like it was nothing.

Rosa yipped. "Put me down. I can walk."

# ZIZI HART

He whispered something in her ear, but we were too far away to hear. Whatever it was, it silenced her.

"What do you think will happen to Rosa?" I asked Dillon.

"Probably WITSEC." Dillon grinned. "I think Taz has found a new pet."

"Don't let Rosa hear you say that." I laughed. "Not sure Taz knows what he's getting into with that one."

"He seems to be doing ok."

"That's only because she's in shock."

"Who has Ramón?" I asked.

We went around the warehouse as men were being arrested, but we couldn't find the kid. Several vans were filling up to take them in for questioning. I watched as they counted the bricks of white powder. It looked like over 100 kilos of cocaine. The pile of weapons was impressive as well. Dillon went off to talk to the DEA agent in charge. I went over to the paramedics to get my arm bandaged up. A few agents and officers were getting treated as well. The member of SWAT Luís had shot looked more annoyed than hurt. The bullet had hit his vest, and he had a substantial bruise blooming on his chest.

"I'm fine. Stop fussing." The guy said to the female paramedic as she applied ice to his bruise. "The guys are already gonna razz my ass."

I grinned. Typical SWAT attitude. Although, I doubt I'd be much better.

"So, what have we got here?" the paramedic asked me as she ripped the sleeve off my bloody shirt, exposing the damage.

I glanced at the wound. It was more of a graze. The bullet looked like it sliced clean through.

"This might need stitches. She pointed to another ambulance. They are doing runs to the hospital in town."

I glanced at the name on her badge. "Listen Sarah, that's not happening."

# SANTA FE SEDUCTION

There was no way in hell I was going to sit at the hospital for hours for a couple of stitches. The only thing I wanted to do was fill out my report and get back to see Mari.

"You refusing treatment?" She asked with a raised brow.

"Just patch me up, so I don't bleed everywhere."

She rolled her eyes. "Fine."

Sarah wiped the wound with antiseptic.

I think she was rubbing harder on purpose. I bit back my groan.

"Are you a sadist?" I asked.

She sighed. "No. But apparently most of the officers here are masochists."

"Yes, we are." I grinned.

After packing the gauze in the wound and wrapping my arm, she sent me on my way.

Scanning the scene, it looked like no one from our side had gotten seriously injured, while the bad guys had massive casualties. Nearly half had been shot. Five of Luís' men were sprawled on the cement, and another six from the supply trucks. All dead. The rest were being treated for injuries and then shipped off to be booked. Dillon stormed back to me clearly pissed off.

"The DEA said they have everything covered. They are sending me home. Me and most of the Narcotics unit. Those pricks. I brought this to them. Typical fucking feds. Taking all the credit."

"What does your Sergeant say?"

"He doesn't have any. Our Captain is here, and he's trying not to ruffle any feathers with the feds." He sighed. "Come on. Let's get out of here."

We walked over to his car. I pulled the phone from my back pocket. The screen was smashed.

"Can you send a text to my family?"

"Already done. They know we're safe."

# ZIZI HART

"Good. Can we swing by the club before heading to mi Mamá's?" I asked Dillon as he made his way through the gambit of vehicles on the scene.

"What could you have there that's so important?"

"My duffel has my shaver and a change of clothes." I pointed at my face. "Mi mamá doesn't like the scruff. And I don't need her seeing me in a bloody shirt."

"Uh huh. It's your mom and not Mari that you're cleaning up for."

"Mi mamá will send you packing if you aren't presentable for almuerzo de Domingo." I chuckled. "No tamales for you."

He perked up. "Irene's tamales? Why didn't you say so?" Dillon turned down the road to the club. Patrol was there. I stripped off the bloody shirt and grabbed the bag from my trunk. I nodded to the officer guarding the entrance.

She stared at my bare chest. Mouth hanging open.

"I need to change inside. Do you mind?"

Dillon shook his head. "Officer Anderson, I think I see some drool there."

She snapped to attention and turned to him.

"Detective." She wiped her mouth.

It earned a chuckle from me.

I changed into a polo and khaki's and shaved off my stubble. I rubbed my hand down smooth cheeks. I hadn't been clean shaven in months. But I needed to shed my past.

Even Dillon changed his shirt and splashed some water on his face. Jac had always been fastidious, even as kids. He had been rolling around on the warehouse floor with the rest of us during the bust, and the guy didn't have a spec of dirt on him. I kind of hated him for that. As we made ourselves presentable, we talked about the feast awaiting us, or moments from the bust, but I knew we were both thinking about the women in our lives. Wanting to see them. Jac had grown up with me, so he was family. He was more like a brother, than a friend. We filled out our reports and

# SANTA FE SEDUCTION

sent them in electronically. Jac got into his car and I followed behind him in mine as we drove to mi mamá's house. As we left the city limits of Santa Fe, I said goodbye to Cruz Diaz, the alias I had used off and on for nearly six years. It was strange to let that part of me go. I wondered if Mari would like the real me. Did I even know what that was after all this time?

# Chapter 27

*Mari*

We all heard the crunch of gravel and knew cars were pulling into the driveway. The four of us ran to the front door. César pulled in first, and then Dillon. When he jumped out of his car, I barely recognized him. He looked so different. Clean shaven in khakis and a polo. Even with the tattoos on his arms, he still somehow looked preppy. He wouldn't be out of place walking the campus at ASU. You would never suspect he had worked for a drug lord. Well, I guess that had never been his day job. His sisters had filled me in on a lot of his secrets. But then I had shared some of my own.

Irene gave him one of her enormous hugs. He winced.

"He's been shot." Dillon stated.

Her eyes went wild, and she started speaking Spanish. The words flowed so fast I couldn't catch them all.

"Why would you say that?" César gave Dillon an evil glare.

He shrugged, clearly loving the drama.

"It's a graze, Mamá. I'm fine."

She started punching his arm.

"Ow, Mamá. Other side. That's where I was shot."

# ZIZI HART

She started kissing and smacking him. Alternating the love and discipline. It was hilarious. His sisters weren't much better. Complaining. Hitting. Hugging.

César was staring at me. I stood off to the side, away from his family, wrapping my arms around myself, uncertain how to react, or what to do. I was in a bulky sweatshirt and skinny jeans I had borrowed from Sofía. My hair was a wreck, and I didn't have on a speck of makeup. His mother and sisters had been up with me all night praying for both the boys to come back to us safely. I hadn't grown up religious, but his family was devout Catholic. Gabriela had gifted me one of her rosaries and through the night I had learned the prayers and now knew them by heart. Irene had taken breaks to bake sweets and make coffee, so I was running on pure sugar and caffeine. The atmosphere had been subdued, until Detective Dillon had texted to let us know they were safe. César's phone had been shattered sometime during the bust. But I hadn't heard his voice or seen him with my own eyes. Until that moment, I hadn't felt like I could breathe. Not fully.

After his sisters and mother had finally stopped the hug/slug fest, swearing they were going to kill him for putting them through this, he separated from the tight group and walked to me.

I opened my mouth, but didn't know what to say. He took me into his arms and kissed me. In front of his family, and his best friend. On the front porch of his mother's home, for all to see. He didn't stop until Sofía started snickering.

"Let her breathe already." Sofía chuckled. "She's going to suffocate."

He stared into my eyes.

"You look so different." I slid my hands over his smooth cheeks.

"I clean up good." He gave me a devilish grin. "So, you've met my crazy family and survived."

"I like them."

# SANTA FE SEDUCTION

"Then you might be crazy too."

"Crazy in love." I said, biting my lip, wondering what he would say.

"I love you too, Mari. So much." He picked me up and gave me another kiss. My feet were off the ground, so I probably looked ridiculous dangling there, but I didn't care. It felt right being in his arms.

"No kids before marriage Césarito." His mother warned.

We both laughed until tears ran down our cheeks. He had to set me down, we were laughing so hard. Irene was a character, and I realized how much I loved his family too. In the last few days, I had grown to care for them almost as much as César.

"Tamales are ready. Inside everyone." Irene yelled from the doorway.

Jac raced inside with Sofía beside him. Gabriella was nowhere to be seen. She must have headed back in already to take care of the kitten. Miles had already been welcomed into the Ramirez family. He was living like a king these days.

"I'm surprised you're not driving that fancy sport car of yours."

"The one you ran into?"

I shoved his good shoulder. "You never did let me explain. Miles had been under the pedal. He's so tiny. I didn't want to step on him."

"Sorry I was such a jerk."

I wrapped my arms around him, giving him another kiss. "I've got a few ideas how you could make it up to me."

His eyes gleamed. "Later."

César opened the door and we walked together into his mother's home to the scents of spice, and the sound of laughter.

Gabriela was feeding bits of tamale to Miles. There were two open seats at the table for us. Our plates were filled the moment we sat down. I had barely taken my first bite when the questions began.

# ZIZI HART

"So, when's the wedding?" Irene asked.

César smiled. "Shut up Mamá."

She picked up a handful of rice and threw it at him.

"Manners, Césarito."

Dillon chuckled. "Irene never changes."

"What? I see how they look at one another."

"I like summer weddings." Gabriela stated.

"I refuse to wear peach." Sofía said. "Promise me Mari, no peach in the bridal party."

My mouth hung open as I looked back and forth at everyone. César didn't say a thing. He just sat there munching on his tamale, grinning at me.

His mother added more food to my plate. "She needs to eat more. Far too skinny. How can she possibly carry a child? I want grandkids."

"Stop razzing her Mamá. Mari is perfect."

"Hmph." Irene grunted. "Fine."

I laughed. I couldn't help it. I couldn't seem to stop chuckling. His family was nuts.

"She's hysterical." Irene said. "Make her stop."

César kissed me. The laughter died in my throat. I think his family was making lewd suggestions in the background, but I barely heard them. I was drowning in this one perfect kiss. A month ago, I had lost the only family I had left, but in the process of searching for answers, I had somehow gained another one. Maybe this had been Benjie's final gift to me. He had told me New Mexico was a place for fresh beginnings. He was right. In the end, Benjie had changed his life around. Righting wrongs. Leaving his past behind. He had taken a chance. I wanted to do the same with this man by my side. This man I barely knew. Cruz Diaz, the bad boy criminal. César Ramirez, the good guy cop. What was in a name anyhow? Benjie had changed his. I never could have imagined the SOB I bumped into at a drive-thru weeks ago could stir up such feelings. Lust and hate had morphed to love,

# SANTA FE SEDUCTION

but I was done questioning why. Life was too short. I had a lifetime to figure out who he was. Who we were together.

# *Appreciation*

Thank you to everyone in my life who has contributed in one way or another to the writing of this book. My insanity or lack thereof is entirely your fault. Just kidding. I appreciate your acceptance of me just as I am, and allowing me to bury myself in my office/cave and not come out for days on end. To my parents, kids, and friends for your support, and endless supply of laughter that keeps me going. To my fellow author friends who understand that writing is our therapy and for being my sounding board whenever I need it. I'm amazed and humbled by your creativity and so grateful for your friendship. And lastly, for those within my inner circle that join me on the journey into the depths of the villain psyche. You always have a rope ready to pull me out if I ever go too far. I owe you more than you can ever imagine.

## *About the Author*

Zizi Hart likes to sprinkle sizzle on her sass. Her muse takes her down shadowed, twisted paths, into her imagination and if you are brave enough to join her on the journey, you won't be disappointed. She writes a mix of fantasy, romance, science fiction, suspense, and adventure, wherever her muse takes her. But no matter what, you will always get a touch of humor and a feel-good story with a lot of heart. In her off-time, she travels the world connecting with nature and animals, getting distracted by decadent chocolates and is forever in search of the perfect brownie sundae.

www.ZiziHart.com

*Thanks for reading!*
***Please add a short review on Amazon.***
*I'd love to hear your thoughts!*

Made in the USA
Monee, IL
11 May 2024